TAR SPACKLED BANNER

A sequel/prequel to
Arboretum: A Utopia

by
J. A. Ellis

Edited by James R. Hugunin

Journal of Experimental Fiction #58

JEF Books
Depth Charge Publishing
Geneva, Illinois

ISBN 1-884097-58-8
ISBN-13 978-1-884097-58-4

ISSN 1084-547X

The Journal of Experimental Fiction
"The foremost in fiction"

TAR SPACKLED BANNER

Two texts hailing from the future were found in the mid-nineties. It's now obvious these texts are apocryphal, but when they were first discovered, the jury was still out.

Popular culture had been mining the topic of time travel for over a two decades in film — *Somewhere in Time* (1980), *Back to the Future* (1985), *Bill and Ted's Excellent Adventure* (1989), and *12 Monkeys* (1995) — and in televison — "The Time Tunnel" (1966), "Quantum Leap" (1989), and "Early Edition" (1996).

In academia, there was a parallel renewal of interest in time, history and narrative, in the phenomenology of retention and and protension in the work of such thinkers as Augustine, Bergson, Husserl, Heidegger, Ricoeur, Merleau-Ponty, Levinas, Derrida, and Deleuze.

So whether an actual artifact from the future or not, I thought one text "timely" enough for reader interest and published it as *Aboretum: A Utopia* in a small comb-bound edition as part of my on-going U-Turn Monograph Series in 1996. The passage of time has proved it to be merely a mockumentary of the future. I have reproduced a page from that text subheaded "Beginnings" and a color map of Arboretum's Capitol City, "Da Clearin'," in pages that follow.

The second text, a prequel/sequel to *Arboretum* and equally a fake, I felt was interesting enough to reader's today despite its wholly fictional depiction of America's troubled future. And so HERE IT IS.

— J. R. H., Oak Park, IL

ARBORETUM

Beginnings   And then. Blargh! Weekly snail-mail delivery came 2 days late. Fewer bloodstains on the envelopes than norm. Plinko! The letter I desired was under Norris Vigilante Service's bill. Sent "tra aero posto," it was postmarked "Da Clearin', Arboretum, Nordo Usonia, 25 oktobro 2053" (3 weeks ago); surrounding the date was a triangle-within-a-triangle in which a drawing of a twig underlined the cancellation's blurb "Estas Heap Bele"—Ar(bor)got for "It's quite fine"—in a font similar to an old 20th-century typewriter. The envelope was delicate, yellowish, and strangely foreign, like mail from Eastern Europe prior to the Big Melt-Down of 2007 at the Walensa Nuclear Power Plant in Wroclaw, Poland that killed the aging experimental theater producer, Jerzy Grotowsky and 30.5 million other Poles and assorted nationalities. (In Arboretum I would learn that their paper stock was completely re-recycled 'nova-papero' that conserved wood.)

Ignoring the gunshots outside, I opened the envelope and gingerly unfolded the even flimsier letter, oriented in horizontal 'landscape' format *[cropped version below(Ed.)]*. It hailed from the Minister of Population and Immigration:

```
23 oktobro 42 P.F./2053\

Da Ministreo o' Logantaro & Enmigrantaro
Sro. Johano Permisos, Komisaro
2300 Strato Fonto, Branch 112
Da Clearin', Arboretum, Nordo Usonia 97205-3345


Kara Amiko!

        Da branches do bonevas you request to come to Da Clearin'
to be grokin' our heap ideal socio. Your apliko to tour-think our
Branchlando do be affirm at da tip-top levels o' our Forest's
branches, ya grok? Da only restrictions do be ne be bringin' into
Da Branchlando electronic devices, fruits or veggies, nor da
followin' beeches Communitas by Paul and Percival Goodman, Brave
New World by Aldous Huxley, Atlas Shrugged by Ayn Rand, or
Neuromancer by William Gibson, nor any writin's by da fasci-
varmint Mark Durfuherman—severe malpermesis!
        Placi be find enclose your guest ticket; do be give this
to da driver o' your L.L.T., 1 o' our lumberin' loggin' trucks,
which do be pickin' you & da other Uitlanders up when your VTOL-
jet do put down near our bordero (eye-ball da enclose itinerary
& map). Do be dressin' heap doubleplus-varma.
        Dankon fer your intereso en our Branchlando,

Sincere via,

Johano Permisos


    "ALTA TO NUN, SURVIVIN' DO BE PREVENTIN' US FROM LIVIN'"
```

Page from J. A. Ellis's *Arboretum*

Map of Arboretum's Capitol City

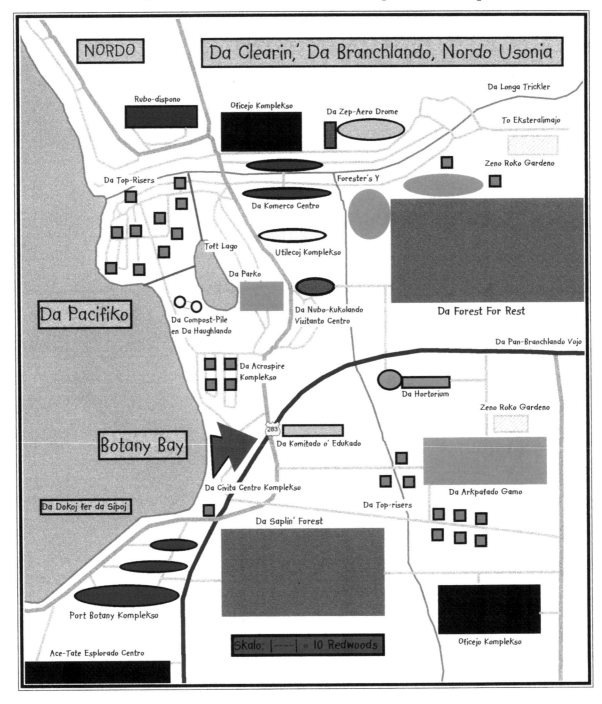

NORDO

Da Clearin,' Da Branchlando, Nordo Usonia

Da Longa Trickler

Rubo-dispono

Oficejo Komplekso

Da Zep-Aero Drome

To Eksteralimajo

Zeno Roko Gardeno

Da Top-Risers

Forester's Y

Da Komerco Centro

Toft Lago

Utilecoj Komplekso

Da Parko

Da Pacifiko

Da Compost-Pile en Da Haughlando

Da Nubo-Kukolando Vizitanto Centro

Da Forest For Rest

Da Pan-Branchlando Vojo

Da Acrospire Komplekso

Da Hortorium

Zeno Roko Gardeno

Botany Bay

283

Da Komitado o' Edukado

Da Civita Centro Komplekso

Da Arkpafado Gamo

Da Dokoj fer da Sipoj

Da Top-risers

Da Saplin' Forest

Port Botany Komplekso

Skalo: |----| = 10 Redwoods

Oficejo Komplekso

Ace-Tate Esplorado Centro

Globo-Com's Satellite Network

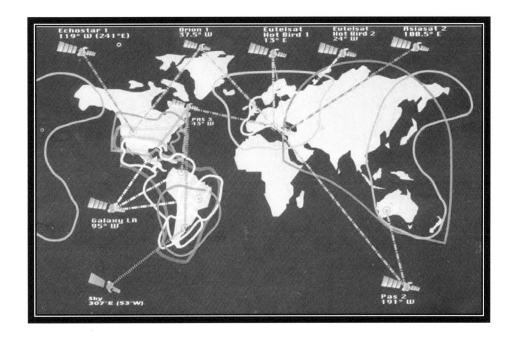

Front cover: *Johns' Flag Pollocked* (2028) from the "Revenge of the Action Painters" series by "Freedom" Trumpoulos, *a.k.a.* William Charles Kile.

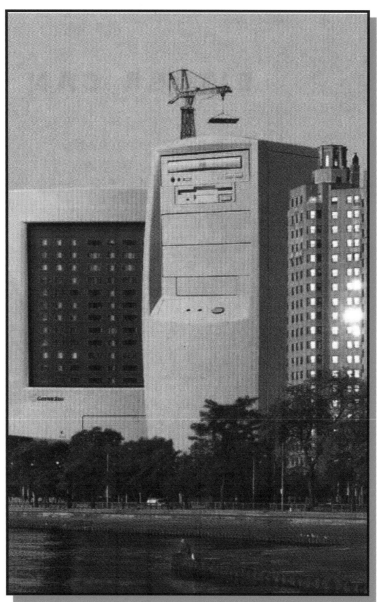

Globo-Com Headquarters, Ascension Island,
Project architect: Mark McVay, Jr.

Nova Republik of Texas's Infamous Flag of Secession (2020)

Only look about you: blood is being spilled in streams, and in the merriest way, as though it were champagne.
—Dostoevsky, *Notes from Underground*

Editor's Introduction

Two years ago Laura, a friend of mine, was cleaning a studio space she'd just rented in Pilsen, southwest of Chicago's famous Loop. There she discovered two manuscripts (one large, one smaller), digital prints, and odd computer diskettes accompanied by a publisher's rejection letter all secreted away on the dusty top shelf of a bookcase—next to a dessicated, dead rat. All were stuffed inside an opened, resealed, blood-smeared padded manila envelope addressed to one "J. A. Ellis, Chicagary, North Usonia" and post-marked, astonishingly, "June 20, 2054." Sender? The return address claimed "Alfred Knopf-Abbeville Press, New Yorsey, North Usonia."

Texts from the future returned by a publishing house that in our time is two distinct entities? A hoax? If not, a future history (an oxymoron?) of the *United* States *in extremis* had been found. According to this text the USA, rife with separatist violence, was renamed Usonia in 2019 ("The Bunker State" or "The Divided States of America" to dissidents) and contrasted markedly with a small ecological utopia known as Arboretum ("Da Branchlando" to its Green citizenry). A surprising revelation of things to come might be in our hands.

But no surprise that despite an exhaustive search, Laura and I could not find the author to get permission to publish the manuscripts. After much urging by Laura, I edited the earlier, larger text down in size, snipping large sections of redundant material. I included bracketed, italicized explanatory editorial comments (I keep the practice here in Ellis's prequel to the larger book) and self-published this redacted version as *Arboretum: A Utopia* (U-Turn Monograph Series #8, 1996).

This larger text, dated earlier than the second, describes in detail Ellis's journey in November, 2053 to a small "ecotopian" sector of North Usonia, formerly the State of Oregon. It had been given over in 2019 A.D. as a land grant to one Charles Cane Forester and his North Usonia Loyalist Alliance Freedom Brigade of anti-fascist freedom fighters after their suppression of the infamous Durfuherman Rebellion. These earlier events are detailed in this, Ellis's second text. The revolt, spurred on by The Nova Republik of Texas's successful bid for autonomy in 2020 A.D. (flag reproduced herein), instigated the bloody secession of Idaho, Montana, and Wyoming from Usonia proper. With global warming making Usonia's south and midwest less habitable and arable, these northern territories became prime real estate. They had to be reclaimed at any cost. The liberal personages who volunteered for that famous Brigade—for instance, the members of famous The Bread and Puppet Theater—were at first defeated at the battle known as "Retreat from Yellow Pine," then victorious at "Wipe out at Warren Ridge," only to be betrayed at "Li'l Intrigue at Big Creek," until finally renewing their forces for the final drive to complete victory at "Return to the River of No Return."

TAR SPACKLED BANNER

According to Ellis first text, Arboretum prides itself in being an "eco-logically post-modem" society in which "da branches" (citizens) have rejected the computer and the Internet ("Just be do sayin' Nyet, ya grok?"); instead, they worship trees and squirrels, love fishing, prefer to abuse marijuana and the flammable element cesium, write chalkboard poetry, and believe in Zenecology, Bokononism, or Chaos Magic. Although rich in detail, this stranger in a strange land's tale appears to a clever travesty past utopias, including Ernst Callenbach's ideal vision in his 1975 novel *Ecotopia*; moreover, it only sketchily fleshs out the author's own personal history. In *Arboretum,* one is forced to read between the lines to glean more about the author's Generation-XX personality and its intersection with the social context of his twlight years in the emergent modes of production and social relations of the Usonian "Bunker State." A time when the Generation XXXers of *Arboretum* were still only teenagers.

An event, astounding as it is improbable, has now allowed us greater insight into Ellis's—as contemporary theory demands we phrase it— *situatedness as a subject* both within Usonia's past (our present) and within the aging Generation-XXers emergence into a Generation-XXX world (our far future). The event? The unexpected arrival of a new manuscript by Ellis written *after Arboretum,* but reworked from memories recalled and diary entries written *prior* to that travelogue. An autobiographical confessional that is, paradoxically, both a sequel and "prequel" to *Arboretum* whose primary material was *experienced* prior to that utopic travelogue, but (supposedly) *re-verified* by time travel.

Laura, prone to Existentialist interpretations, said its form and content reminded her of Dostoevsky's *Notes from Underground.* Ellis exhibits his consciousness, like "the underground man," as an "intensively developed individuality," she said. Bolstered her argument by noting that in *Arboretum*: "Ellis tells how government offices had literally, due to the violence of the neo-Fascist 'Troubles,' gone underground; how Ellis observes his own monkish existence from behind bullet-marked walls, escaping via virtual reality when younger and via illegal time travel as an adult."

I disagreed. Oh granted, Ellis was an isolated, lonely man—after all, he is/was/will be (?) a writer-teacher, a target for every kook and disgruntled student—and, sure, the snow he describes outside his Chicagary flat is, as in Dostoevsky's *Notes,* dingy, yellow, wet. But the latter is a fact not a symbol. It is a realist description of the result of acid rain and the near-bursting bladders of the millions of homeless/evicted that can't be chalked up to spleen. In the second text, Ellis dreams/ dreamed/will dream (?) of a new Society of Friendliness to All in which cultural production would become "infectious" as Leo Tolstoy termed it, uniting humankind. Ellis's exposition implicity reiterates a question once posed by black activist Michele Wallace: "Where is tomorrow's avant-garde in art and entertainment to take on the racial bias of the snowblind, the sexual politics of the frigid, and the class anxieties of the perennially upper crust?" ("Reading 1966 and The Great American Whitewash," in *Remaking History*, 1989). In the first text, Ellis finds it in his sojourn to ecotopic Arboretum.

"But," Laura countered, "Ellis, like the underground man, rallies against the usual conceptions of the New Eden. He attacks the ills of urbanism, Positivist rationalization, and Behaviorist manipulation. He sets himself against, as the underground man puts it, the socius as 'anthill and chicken coop.' Ellis, I think, is seeking an anarchic existential freedom that, just to assert itself, may seemingly choose the irrational against more rationalistic alternatives. Hence, his approval of the Arboretian dissidents "Da Hobos."

I disagreed. Ellis's theory of his own subjectivity was more informed by a postmodernist anti-Humanism that rejects the "anti-hero" and revels in "the death of the author." *In the Beginning was the Word, and now there's only the Quote.* So I vote: no Sartre or Camus here; more a "lying autobiography" as James Joyce's brother, Stanisluaus, once called *Portrait of the Artist as a Young Man.* Did not Ellis teach/taught/will teach (?) Advanced Plagiarism? Did he not think/thought/will think (?) of "copyright" as "the right to copy?" Did he not hold his own against the indigenous inhabitants in *Arboretum* when "Playin' Jarism," a form of "ventriloquism" in which one makes obscure textual references and blatant citations without giving authorial credit? For Ellis, the question is not *To be or not to be,* but *To read or to be read.* Is there nothing outside the text how does one write a better future? Hence, his curiosity, his impatience, his desire to visit Arboretum, a "real-existing" (if we believe him) hodgepodge of a utopia cobbled together from past utopias. *Arboretum* details something of that desire and records his adventures in "Da Branchlando." *Tar Spackled Banner*, the second text, sketches in the personal and social background to that travelogue.

You're thinking how had it come into my possession and why dare publish it? *Possession is ninetenths the law* in capitalist societies, you know.

As a professor of art history, freelance critic, and cottage-industry publisher who also dabbles in international short-wave listening—which puts me in touch with staff from many foreign radio stations as well as a few reprobates who pilfer the mails then direct strange requests or abusive comments to the unfortunate whose return address they so obtain—I often receive peculiar and arcane items in my mailbox. Little did I know that the little benign notice from the college mailroom informing me in red felt-tip pen that:

> THERE'S A PACKAGE FOR YOU IN THE MAILROOM

would lead to confirming either: 1) a strange a person from the future had been among us; or, 2) a rip in the fabric to time had propelled two manuscripts back to us here and now; or, 3) we were simply being hoaxed by some very clever, but unlucky, operator working out of Ankara, Turkey.

THE EVIDENCE

**P.O. Box - 333 -
06.443 Yenişehir
ANKARA-TÜRKIYE**

**LOGO, RETURN ADDRESS, AND THE
STAMPS AFIXED TO THE PACKAGE**

I handed the mail guy the yellow card, retrieving a card-board box with a return address sporting the official logo of the short-wave radio station "The Voice of Turkey" (VOT). Upon opening, it exuded an unpleasant odor—strong coffee blended with chain-smoked cigarettes—and contained an inner package one-inch thick and wrapped in crispy light brown paper of obvious foreign origin. Carefully opening the package, it was slightly damaged in shipment, I discovered the this second manuscript neatly typed on foreign format paper. Inside, a lonely scrap of paper upon which the phrase "Don't be deceived" (the Arboretian dissidents' rallying cry) had been hand-scrawled in blue ink in Ar(bor)got, Arboretum's wacky hodgepodge lingo composed of Ebonics, Slango, Novo Vorto, and Esperanto:

Be ne trompis!

On the reverse side of this paper scrap, a fragment of typed text survived from another purpose to tease my speculations as to its possible source:

> Amis lecteurs:
>
> Dans notre édition du mois dernier, vous avez certainement remarqué le grand nombre d'erreurs de grammaire et de fautes de frappe qui émaillaient la première partie de notre conte. C'est par inadvertance de notre part que ce texte n'a pas été soumis . . .

This text appears to be an official apology for grammatical errors in some past edition of an unknown publication, most likely one by External Service of the Voice of Turkey. Other clues were the Turkish stamps and the hand-printing on the mailing envelope matching that found on the note inside. Was Ellis, or whoever was posing as him, working for The Voice of Turkey?

Where to start? The return address. I wrote back to The Voice of Turkey, making appropriate inquiries. Thirty-three days later I received a terse note (on VOT letterhead) in awkward English denying any knowledge of said package. Paradoxically, as if denying their denial, enclosed was a front page news item with photographs from a Turkish daily; translated from Turkish it read:

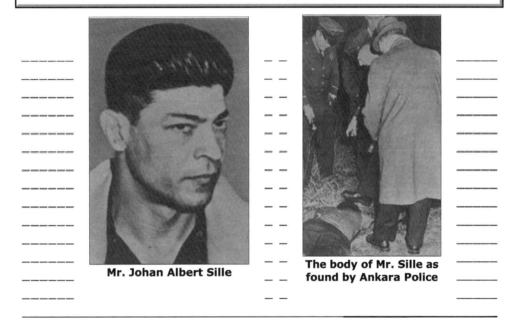

MYSTERIOUS 'VOT' MYSTERY MAN DIES MYSTERIOUSLY

Mr. Johan Albert Sille

The body of Mr. Sille as found by Ankara Police

I had the accompanying article translated and give only the gist of the event here: "Johan Albert Sille *[J.A. Ellis?]*, a writer recently hired by the External Service of The Voice of Turkey, but of whom little is known, was run down by a hit-and-run driver after coming out of a post office in Ankara. The driver, according to one witness, sped away from the scene in a Ford pickup truck with "AmPat"—abbreviation for the American Patriots, a Usonian Right-wing extremist group mentioned in *Arboretum*—painted on its side in red, white, and blue. The police, unfamiliar with this insignia from the future, must have thought it was a ploy to confuse identification.

Another witness mentioned seeing a blonde female passenger in the vehicle, but this could not be confirmed." One station employee was cited as having the impression, "Sille was a loner" and noted that "he kept to himself."

Curiously, the employee thought it pertinent to point out that "he always had a copy of Claude Lévi-Strauss's *Tristes Tropiques* on his desk."

The manager at his hotel said was "polite, but prone to arguments" and noted that "he once surprised me by yelling what I thought were "Italian or Portuguese"—mostly likely Ar(bor)got—epithets at a mysterious Oriental-looking visitor who was leaving his apartment in great haste, carrying a chess board under his arm." The description of this other man jived with that of Sako Mako, the sly Usonian C.I.A. collaborator with whom Ellis played chess in *Arboretum.* Police investigation of Sille's premises "turned up nothing unusual."

J.A. Sille's Thumb Print

Nevertheless, I FAXed the Ankara Police to inquire more specifically into this man's possessions, feigning that I possibly knew him, knowing that what they'd see as unremarkable, I might find extremely informative. Their return FAX meticulously provided a picture of a police lab technician holding an enlargement of Sille's thumbprint and detailed both expected and unexpected items like a used jalapeño-green condom found in the bathroom's waste-basket. I will only share with you several items that caught my eye. Two passports. One or both under (I assume) an assumed name. One was issued in the United States in 1994 to Johan Albert Sille; the other . . . did I dare believe my eyes . . . issued in 2050 in Usonia to a John Avery Ellis! The former showed trips had been made between 1994 - 1995 to the U.S.A., Portugal, Austria, and Australia; while the latter recorded a visit to Arboretum, North Usonia in 2053! Also found: 1) a small plastic pin-hole camera; 2) an unusual PowerBook, hard-drive wiped clean as a whistle; 3) a post card featuring Chicago's famous skyline (I wondered if it was a future vista altered by the presence of the terrorist-damaged Miglin-Beitler Tower leaning crazily like the Tower of Pisa, a scene described by Ellis/Sille in both his texts); 4) a small, well-worn digitally-scanned photo of two men, one black, standing in front of a neon sign for THE SMOG-CUTTER LOUNGE. In the man's bookcase were found hardbacks, brittle with age: the collected works of Spanish philosopher-novelist Miguel de Unamuno, Laura Gilpin's famous photo book *The Enduring Navajo,* Stephanie Kaza's *The Attentive Heart: Conversations with Trees,* an Esperanto grammar text, and a dictionary of colloquial Navajo. In addition, several dog-eared, yellowing paperbacks were

Cover, Pau D'Arco's
Basco's Dilemma(1996)

discovered: Ernst Callenbach's *Ecotopia,* Arboretum's founder Charles Cane Forester's classic *Da Green Book,* Charlotte Perkins Gilman's *Herland,* Carl C. Pfieffer's *The Schizophrenias: Yours and Mine,* Aristophanes's *Lysistrata,* Rabelais' *Gargantua and Pantagruel,* a John Barth novel on audiotape I've not heard of (has it even been written yet?) titled *She Seas Anenomously*, Italo Calvino's *If on a Winter's Night a Traveler,* a Do-It-Yourself book on building geodesic dome-homes, and (surprise, surprise!) Pau D'Arco's *Basco's Dilemma*, the odd text Ellis/Sille mentions in *Arboretum* and the subject of his in-progress scholarly monograph, a biography of Basco Da Lemma, the Portuguese-American founder of The Society of Friendliness to All (SOFTA). The Ankara Police sent me Ellis/Sille's copy, which they'd found on a coffee table next to four bound Xerox texts of old hard backs checked out from two institutions on, respectively, July 5th and July 7th, 2053! The first two—a Naturalist's manual on reptiles and salamanders, and a basic botany textbook—were stamped in green ink:

The third and fourth—a compact, undated volume of C.C. Bombaugh's *Oddities and Curiosities of Words and Literature (Gleanings for the Curious),* and a very slim scholarly study, Bergen Evans's *The Psychiatry of Robert Burton* (1944)—sported in Chicago Bulls-red ink on the inside front covers:

Curiously, also discovered was a rare, valuable copy of the Icelandic tale *The Saga of Gunnlaug Serpent-tongue* as translated and illustrated by William Morris and printed in a limited edition in 1869 in a replica of Caxton typeface by Chiswick Press. The Ankara Police sent a Xerox copy of a page from the book:

The story of Gunnlaug the Worm-tongue and Rafen the Skald. Even as Ari Thorgilson the learned, the priest, hath told it. Who was the man of all Iceland most learned in tales of the land's inhabiting and in lore of time agone.

Chapter i. Of Thorstein Egilson and his Kin.

There was a man called Thorstein, the son of Egil the son of Skallagrim, the son of Kveldulf the Herse, of Norway. Asgerd was the mother of Thorstein: she was the daughter of Biorn Hold. Thorstein dwelt at Burg in Burg-firth: he was wealthy of fee, and a great chief, a wise man, meek and of measure in all ways. He was nought of such wondrous growth and strength as his father Egil had been: yet was he a right mighty man, and much beloved of all folk. Thorstein was goodly to look on, flaxen-haired, and the best-eyed of men: and so say men of lore that many of the kin of the Mere-

a i   men

A page from Ellis's copy of *The Saga of Gunnlaug Worm [Serpent]-tongue*

This saga is a curious one. Gunnlaug, "a rather libellous" serpent-tongued poet—

> *I of the Serpent's [or "worm's"] tongue,*
> *Name earned when I was young, may prove thy bane.*

—was an actual historical personage (his verse appears in *The Skalds* translated by Lee M. Hollander, published for The American-Scandinavian

TAR SPACKLED BANNER

Foundation by Princeton University Press, 1947). He and his rival in words and love, Hrafn, fight with swords over Helga—"the loveliest woman there has ever been in Iceland." Hrafn is killed. Gunnlaug, mortally wounded by Hrafn's treachery, dies soon afterwards. Later, Gunnlaug appears to Illugi the Black in a dream and says:

> *One blow I got from Hrafn's blade,*
> *One blow, and all my debts were paid.*
> *Yet, my own sword struck him where he stood*
> *And Hrafn needs must wade in blood.*

Helga marries another, dying later still in love with Gunnlaug—"And Helga's death seemed a very great loss, as was to be expected."

Why did Ellis have the text? An investment? Maybe there some relevance here to Ellis's own life—a love lost? Or is the connection between the violence in the saga and the violence in Ellis's own society? Does the saga mime aspects of Ellis's own text? After all the saga has been shown to have confusing chronology, and there is considerable doubt about the authenticity of the verses voiced by Gunnlaug within the narrative—it is known that one, at least, is attributed to another poet besides Gunnlaug.

Very slim evidence from which to make profound deductions. But enough to, at least, convince Laura and I that the deceased, Johan Albert Sille, had been John Avery Ellis, the mystery author of *Arboretum*. But whether Ellis/Sille was a visitor from our future or not, whether his texts were pure fabulations or an accurate histories—the question remains open-ended.

As for its autobiographicalness, did Ellis/Sille's second text pass French critic Philippe Lejeune's definition of it as "A retrospective account in prose that a real person makes of his own existence stressing his individual life and especially the history of his *[sic]* personality*[?]*" Only if one adds *imagery* after "prose" as the media and assumes Ellis to be *a real person*.

I argued that, given our postmodern times, with its heightened consciousness of knowledge as constructed and provisional, such a question pertaining to *real person* and *veracity* was moot, that it's only by an act of faith that one can sustain the claim or the belief that a text one is reading is an autobiography. "We used to," I explained, "take the *autos* (the self) of autobiography as unproblematic, neutral, and only examine whether the *bios* (the life) was accurately reflected by the *graphē* (the writing). We no longer take *autos* as unproblematic, nor do we believe *graphē* can be a one-to-one correspondence with external fact. Neither the *auto* nor the *bios* is there in the beginning, a completed entity to be had for the taking. All we have now are 'fictions of the self' as Michael Sprinker has put it." I smiled, licked my right index finger and made an invisible digital stroke in the air before my surprised friend's face.

"Uh . . . Perhaps it's more relevant to say that the autobiographer half discovers, half creates a deeper design and truth than adherence to historical and factual truth could ever make a claim to?" she replied softening her position, a bit taken aback by my astute remarks.

Laura went on to speculate that Ellis/Sille's interest in his own life demonstrates that even in the near future with VR-tripping ubiquitous and the horde-mentality of recombinant fascism posing as libertarianism and spreading its ugly stain across Usonia, there will remain a fascination with the self and its profound and endless mysteries—albeit accompanied by an anxiety about that very self as rooted in the dim and vulgar entity known as "The Bunker State."

She then looked at the text from another angle, starting from Ellis/Sille's theoretical activities, saying that a critic—such as Ellis/Sille—is really a closet autobiographer, citing two authorities on the issue. Nietzsche: "Little by little it has become clear to me that every great philosophy has been the confession of its maker, as it were his involuntary and unconscious autobiography." Paul Valéry: "There is no theory that is not a fragment, carefully prepared, of some autobiography." And that Ellis/Sille's confession here achieves completeness as a conversion narrative by recording the death of the old individual (the young 'trode-headed Ellis, the dryasdust "acanemic" addicted to "the already-written and-seen" prior to his visit to Arboretum) and his replacement by the new self-critical person (Ellis after his visit to that utopia): "For haven't we already seen in *Arboretum* that Ellis/Sille will start to bring the creative act of autobiography into his future criticism and criticism into his autobiographical travel sketches?"

Concerning travel, Laura claimed that: "Ellis/Sille was totally PC 'cause he chose to live sporadically in a 'Third World' country like Turkey and had a romantic attachment to the memory of his buddy 'Don-de-bartender' who died fighting for Turkey's sovereignty."

Yet, I argued, the author, an expert in plagiarism, might have been equally attracted there as significant scenes from William Gibson's cyberpunk novel *Neuromancer* take place in Turkey. I was not swayed by Laura. Sure, I *wanted* to believe Ellis/Sille. I wanted to take as a sign of the future his peculiar diction and vocabulary, replete with the suffix "*eroo*" (which convincingly hints at either mass migrations of Australian hackers to Usonia or the importation of Australian films in vaster numbers in our future). But all the physics I had learned mitigated against Ellis/Sille's claims to have jerry-rigged a 2052 Maytag clothes dryer into a low-tech time-machine. *That* sounded more like a bad pastiche of either very bad 1930s Sci-Fi or a keen appreciation of early 1950s Sci-Fi TV kids programs (*Space Patrol* or *Captain Video and his Video Rangers*).

TAR SPACKLED BANNER

Ellis/Sille, sensitive to the fact that the formalities and franchises of history are now seen by Progressives as displaced into a dispersal of stories, provides us with a chorus of personal commentaries, a crowd of personal reckonings: a self composed of many social roles, many personae as intuited by Gurdjieff and given rigorous theoretical exposition during the "elder-age," Ellis's hacker term for the 1980-90s. Ellis is a *discontinuous* self that refuses to be totalized. He thinks in other heads; and in his own, others besides himself think.

J.A. Ellis at home (2029)

Even the best photograph he supplied of himself, where he gazes distractedly out his kitchen window, reveals little. Ellis/Sille builds his decentered self-portrait within the full knowledge of three attacks on the unity of the individual: 1) Descartes' apprehension of his *I think* within the enunciation of the nihilating *I doubt*; 2) Freud's positing the self as split between conscious and unconscious: *Here in the field of dreams, you are at home*; and, 3) Jacques Lacan's reading of Freud's unconscious as constituting us in language, we are inscribed within The Symbolic.

Moreover, in a section devoted to his "gradpup" seminar concerning his own sobful "mourning feelosofy" (pages 76 - 79)—an ontology of decline touting the death of metaphysics—we discover Ellis/Sille's rétro-indebtedness to "elder-day" Italian "Weak Thought" *alla* Gianni Vattimo, Giovanna Borradori, and Pier Aldo Rovatti. Ellis/Sille's confessional focuses on the process and not just the moment, on the scene and not just the individual, on the body and not just the figure. His very digressions, his autobiography-as asymptotic-function, tells us he's aware that "The Bunker State's" culture of the self is central to neo-liberal illusions of democracy that wants people to consume and that, by doing so,

Workers in The Bunker State

fosters bogus authenticity by reducing everything to slogans, identity-bytes and publicity images. Moreover, this asymptote-of-the-self finds its social counterpart in the expression of a utopic desire (what might be) for an all-inclusive democratic future, a Society of Friendliness to All. Ellis/Sille wonders if such might not be found in Arboretum, what its citizens call in Ar(bor)got: "Da Branchlando o' Nordo Usonia."

TAR SPACKLED BANNER

Zenecological monk in conversation with a tree

Because of this utopic desire toward an all-inclusive society, Ellis/Sille delves into Zenecology (rooted in Zen monk Stephanie Kaza's *The Attentive Heart: Conversations with Trees*) and its adversaries—"recombinant fascism" and the "blarghful pan-capitalism" underwritten by the pro-corporate neo-liberalism of the Francis Fukuyama (see *The End of History and the Last Man,* 1992) and Luc Ferry ilk—ideological conflicts that escalated into bloody conflicts that plagued his formative years as a "Komputerkind" in San Angelo (formerly Los Angeles).

The latter's rétro-existentialist thought undermines Arboretum's founding principle as expressed by the slogan on their flag: *Uti Non Abuti*—literally meaning "Use, Don't Abuse," which those Arboretians translate punfully "Tre(e)at With Repect." In *The New Ecological Order* (1995), Ferry attacks deep ecologies such as Zenecoogy as "a new cosmology," and, in opposition to it touts culture that tears itself *away* from nature; culture is to be positively measured by the distance it maintains from nature. He, thus, impugns a Zenecology based on decentering the human subject and bringing a *rapprochement* between subject

Arboretian Eco-Love Fest

and object, going so far as to claim deep ecology has fascistic and communistic aspects; this he then counters with vague and outmoded concepts ringing of individual freedom and democracy that mask corporate greed. At best, he can

Entrance to Arboretum

only muster a soft eco-reformism based on global consensus about emissions, toxic waste, clean water, etc., which doesn't alter the modes of thought that produce these noxious by-products in the first place.

But I digress. In conclusion, one of the most seminal *and* pregnant books (Laura wanted this praise to be bisexual) in "Postie Lit," *Tar Spackled Banner* is in structure and form one of the most daringly original un-original texts Laura and I've ever read. Aping both Dostoevsky's *Notes from Underground* and, I would add, Thomas Carlyle's *Sartor Resartus,* it mixes those texts with an artist-bookish concern with visual material to an extent that the text doesn't fit literary genres; this scripto-visual production defies easy classification. It is at once a "green book," a philosophical treatise, an autobiography, a romance-of-the-marginal, and an artist book.

As Laura put it: "It's as heady and slippery a cocktail as Ellis/Sille's preferred oily mixed drink—O.J.'s Bronco. Ya grok?" I "grokked." Laura's only disappointment with the text was that Ellis/Sille isn't writing, can't write— despite his scholarly knowledge of "Uterineroo" Aussie-Feminist Theory—from "the femino-engendered space of Middle-aged Womyn, Generation-XX."

Ellis/Sille's text is given here in its entirety, down to all the illustrations supplied by the author. But Laura had argued vehemently for changing the title. She'd felt that it was a misnomer, *spackled* used for what she thought should have been more properly *speckled* or *splattered.* I countered that *spackled* denoted a reparative process which, using tar (which along with feathers was effectively employed by early American revolutionaries), would certainly leave its marks, not hiding the process of restoration (an activity that is usually associated with blue-collar labor). Moreover, I argued, Ellis's most carefully chosen word, *spackled*, would still evoke in the reader's mind those

other related words, *speckled* and *splattered.* Hence, *spackled is a very clever condensation* (a combining of elements into a single sign described by Freud as an aspect found in both dreams and jokes) of all the various meanings constellating around those three terms into a single word. Capitulating to my psychoanalytic reading, Laura finally withdrew her objection.

My editorial comments and clarifications—I've kept them briefer than I did in *Arboretum*—are italicized and within brackets (albeit some are by Ellis). Although *Tar Spackled Banner* is understandable *sans* familiarity with Ellis/Sille's previous text, the reader who wishes to develop a profound understanding of Ellis/Sille and his social *situatedness* should obtain a copy of *Arboretum* and read it prior to launching into this sequel.

—James R. Hugunin, Oak Park, IL

PART ONE

I

The subtler forms of self-deception lie around us, and never do they lie more temptingly at hand than when the subject is our own character with all its merits and the extenuations of its infrequent errors.
—Edgar Johnson, *One Mighty Torrent* (1937)

Dear Peeper: blarghful *[unpleasant]* boredom may lead you to anything, even working up many years of remembrances and diaristic jottings into both personal confession and social indictment. I here play 2 roles: an archivist-time-traveler doing primary research and a synthesizer suturing up the surviving fragments of my life. A life cobbled together using the phraseroos: *moreover, and then*. It is painful re-membering, a putting together of the dis-membered past to make sense of the trauma of the present. Yes, I hear your question: *Why the perennial mañana? Why all this in* 1 mighty torrent—*now? [A reference to a line in a poem by Shelley.]* My excuseroos are excusable.

First. Discomfort and doubt. Most contemporary texts are hypertexts. To redact diary entries for human peepers by hypertexting, that is, max imizing peeperly choices in a life already-lived, presents great difficulty for that form. So must revert to, at best, a dialogic imagination expressed in conventional ways. *Moreover.* To reflect *now* on the *back then*, tempts one to do so for *hysterical reasons*, altering one's observations of *now* in a stupid way for the sake of backwards compatibility with one's past *then*. Plinko! What is lost, put at second remove from origins, is what C.G. Jung dubbed "the terrible ambiguity of an immediate experience." In order to accomplish both of the above, one must first have a mind completely at easeroo and without a trace of doubt left. Yes, yes. Like the *vas bene clausum,* the well-sealed mental vessel, of either the blinkered Fundamentalist or the tenured Humanist acanemic, ya peep?

You laugh? Ha ha only serious! This is an achievement neither pingful *[pleasant]* nor easy in our blarghful *[awful]* Bunker State of Mind (BSM). Discomfort and doubt, twin stars mutually producing the dual-gravities of our society, Usonia, or The Bunker State (TBS) as our Lefties (what's left of them) have dubbed it. Try and escape Doubt, Discomfort pulls one in with increasing force; try and escape Discomfort, Doubt pulls all the harder. Together they increase the magnitude of the levity-quotient needed to reach escape velocity to detach oneself from our de*spic*able Desmodernidad *[the state of living in*

1

permanent chaos, from the Spanish noun desmadre, *meaning to be motherless]*. A State that is all-elbows *[very brusque, disregarding]* with its citizens and their eco-environment.

Moreover. Ugh, bletch! The fear of autobogotiphobia. To take the slack *[hacker jargon for 'internal fragmentation']* of one's life-memories and defrag it is to instantly bogotify *[make bogus, over-simplify]* it. To produce coherence and closure where it probably doesn't existeroo. One risks the production of a personal and familial fakelore. As V.Y. Mudimbe put it: "History is a legend, an invention of the present." *And then.* There's an epiphenomenon of this bogotification process: the tendency towards *creeping elegance,* doting on certain autobiographic points at the expense of the *seemingly* less interesting, but not necessarily less important, parts of one's life-story.

Moreover. Suppressio veri: biography is firmly in the possession of the hack, talk-show host, and spin-doctor—blarghful yak-yaks all with 80-column *[deficient, slow]* minds. The plausible knave and the man of maladroit virtue are on audiotape and cyberspace as well as in the flesh (and the half-flesh of the humanoids). *And then.* Even more unfortunate for my project. *Suggestio falsi*: autobiography is in the hands of everyone. Earth's total communications company, Globo-Com, encourages, nay, *urges,* the proles to have their own personal Websites. (These sites of self-promotion have become so organic to our cyberlives, an insanely great wit once suggested they be redubbed "Web-cytes.") Yes. *Downloadable biobytes for every Beavis and Butthead by every Beavis and Butthead,* goes the Globo-Com jingle. *Pure biodemocratic Level-lution,* claim its supporters. *Pure fritterware,* counter its critics.

Sorry St. Augustine. Confessions no longer in the hands of saints. Sorry Blaise Pascal. *Pensées* replaced by either puffing boasts or self-righteous self-roasts. *O.K.* Marcuse's "affirmative culture" with bang! Maybe an occasional *me-malign* that allows no virtues, no abilities, no merits whatsoever, until the peepers wonder why one ever chose to chronicle a self so mucho the futile clowneroo—the fav neg strategy of our aesthetic Mean-Modemists, our *derrière-garde,* who worship as that proto-derrière-gardist, Paul McCarthy, an artist who irritated the sensibilities of Southern California audiences in the late-20th century. But I do digresseroo.

Genrecide. That's what it is. Traditional confession corrupted by an all pervasive Pop-Modemism with its On-line Personals, Chat Rooms, Hypertexts, and Webcytes. That's why I'm again physically moving backwards in time to script this. Risking the wrath of Usonia's Tempokops who enforce TBS's strict prohibs on temporal-displacement. Although such displacement is relativity easeroo—you rewire a Taco-Bell Maytag industrial-size clothes dryer to revolve opposite the earth's rotation at quadruple its norm r.p.m., install a kill-switch inside rigged to an vintage oven-timer, add a whole box of Taco-Bell Downy's Bounce anti-static dryer sheets to prevent electrocution, and stuff oneself inside after fasting from solid food for 12 hours previous—Usonian propaganda has painted such a bleak cyberpic of the past that most Usitizens *[Usonian citizenry]* have turned to "Chemistry for a Better Future." All manner of Taco-Bell Dow designer drugs. *And then.* One's body can only be displaced *backward*, or forward to the *original* time from which one was displaced. Blargh! Heap no time-travel into one's future, pilgrim. So it's mucho more pingful to forgo the vertigo and walkabout backwarderoo by peeping rétro-vids (like Hitchcock's original *Vertigo*), re-reruns of TV reruns, auditing Oldies-But-Goodies on rare vinyls or tuning in Globo-Com's 24 hour Nostalgia-Tunes Channel, and making Taco-Bell Pillsbury heap rétro-Do-It-Yourself-Again Cake Mix mixes.

So who I am to attempt to revive the genre? Where are my creds? I sport no old-timer's tattoos and skin-piercing holes. A scar from my identichip insertion surgery maybe. That's all. *And why?* you ask. A commemorative instinct fed by self-affection or nostalgia? Dessert for a well-nourished ego? But I'm no Napoleon, with a complaint or interesting story, marooned on a bare rock at St. Helena. Nor am I a sports coach with endorsements to make. A didactic purpose? But I'm no Euripides, a sad old man with a long beard, mind-crunching on something pingfully great and high. An apologia? But *je ne regret rien*—except my birth. I still call my *madre* by the tag *muerte:* by giving me life she gave me death—Q.E.D. Pecuniary reasons? The pan-capitalism logician may so charge, knowing my pedagogic profession is even less valued and more ill-paid in TBS than it was when this gaggleroo of disparate citizenry was called The United States. Nay, gentlefolk! I enclose no contract. I make no endorsements.

Say more fueled by abstract enthusiasms. Devotion to principles and causes that proclaim: *No pingful tranforms of the pan-capitalist economy is possible in the absence of trans-zonal political co-ops by anti-systemic movimientos* (SexDemo Pres., Manuel Wallerez-Stein). *And then.* The pingfully astounding fact that an earlier pingful female resident of a heap tamer Chicagary (it was still dubbed "Chicago" then) had found my, so to yak, ms.-in-a-bottle. She cajoled, complained, seduced to get it published; she defended its fantastic veracity; she touted its mysterious author, me, finally convincing her male art critic friend to put it into hardcopy—*Arboretum.* So, unwittingly, she and he now prompt me to expose my delicate subjectivity and precarious social context in heap deep gratituderoo. Against my cautious and paranoid sensibility—survival habits from living in TBS—I give to your time a present of *my presence* in your future written in your present, my past. Like Ripley, you may believe it or not. Peeper! Peep that thou shalt weep. As the *ecolustreeous* founder of Da Branchlando *[Arboretum]* once wrote in his bozotic ebonic diction: *Da self-confessor's trials in workin' to grok him- or herself now do be becomin' da peeper's trials in makin' sense o' da text* (Charles Cane Forester, *Da Green Book*).   *   *   *

II

Oh hoe sake can U.C. bye to Don's oily light what's a brow delete hail order jai alai's strapped bleeding. Who's brought strikers and stars true 'nuff perish the night, ant farm ramparts we washed while our friends were still weeping. And a rock has a glare in the moon-shiny bright and our friends were still there till their morning's departing. Oh hey dusty sparkly bananas weigh about as much as pears and apples too.
Play ball!
—Eckhard Gerdes, *Ring in a River* (1994)

Blargh! I am a sickeroo . . . I am a spiteful man. I am an unpleasant man. *[Ellis's opening travesties the opening lines of Fyodor Dostoevsky's* Notes from Underground.*]* An over-educated pedagogueroo (I can still do math in my head and rarely use my grammar/spell-check tools on the computer). What novelist Eckhard Gerdes aptly terms an "Acanemic." Aye pilgrim, the diagnosis always precedes the etiological account. Crank *[think]* my lungs are diseaserooed. Too many youngsteroo years inhaling San Angelo Metro Basin's *[Los Angeles Basin]* smogeroo. I'm among 5% of population whose MSG level is blarghfully high, that min-amount mucho can kill us. My kidneys are weak. Bad water. Or too many—weekly, nay, daily—kid-mes over 'O.J.'s Bronco' cocktails at The Smog-Cutter Lounge. A dingy dump on Vermont not far from Chatterton's, my fav old-book-joint in S.A. *[Los Angeles]* where I used to buy *real paper* books—now closed some dozen years. Most reading material only can be had as Hear-Ye audio-tapes, Taco Bell KaPow-R-Bookdisks, and interactive Hypertexto-novellas offered by Globo-Com Net. The entity that post-modemists, negating electro-affirmative culture, badcrit-call "The Nyet." Pingful punful jokeroo too if I weren't so damn-addicted to, so well-netted by, The Net. I can't, as post-modemists suggest, "Just say *Nyet.*"

O.J.'s Bronco? Concocted of

gin   grenadine
juice from a freshly knife-slasherooed orange
stale lemon-juice concentrate
drop of Pennzoil   crushed ice

and deftly done by Don-de-bartender. Those tart 'O.J.'s had us late-afternoon quafferoos—me, "Spuds" Swallough, and "Freedom" Trumpoulos—plastered muchonuff on liquid stufferoo to subversively sing—at real risk of arrest, with Don providing the explanatory chorus—

> Me: *In the dark day!*
> Don: *For dat do been life now.*
> Spuds: *In the bright night!*
> Don: *Da night bright wit black helicopter flood-lights.*
> Freedom: *Oopah! Gathered the brave lads!*
> Don: *Look at dem brave L.A. lads, silent-talkin', sittin'-standin'.*
> *[A travesty of a poem in M.E. Saltykov-Shchedrin's satire* The Swallows.*]*

Afterwards my 2 drinking buddies and I would hail our tender host, 1-man Chorus, and Grand Inquisitor as "Don-de-Tarbucket." A moniker derived from the bozotic-looking military marching hat worn by West Pointeroos, such as Don had once been. His hat, mustard stains still visible, hung over the mirror in his bar next to his framed UCLA E-mailresponse Course Diploma in *The History, Theory, and Praxis of Alcoholic Chemistry and its Diaspora*, 1 of mucho many nova e-mailresponse courses developed to placate the many minority communities after the University of California system eliminated Affirmative Action in the late 1990s for its regular courses of study.

After graduating from an all-black high school in the Compton area where he'd lettered in track—his school-colored bullet-proof vest was on display there in a bullet-proof case until the building was burned down 2 years later by starchy-white AmPats—Don-de-Pacifist had chosen the lesseroo of 2 evils. The military-industrial complex was the voice of moderation *then*. It still pingfully practiced Affirmative Action. He'd won an appointment to West Point to make a point about the gaggleroo of militant Generation-XXer Skinheads that *then* basheroo-dominated the civilian campuses. Like those, I teach by textual example here, that gave that black acanemic, "Chappie" Puttbutt, such a hard time in Ishmael Reed's novel *Japanese By Spring*, ya peep?

No one hates war more than the soldier, or so said Gen. MacArthur once, maybe twice. And Don had believed him. But Don was mustered out his first year—literally, upperclassmen covered him with mustard, or as he put it: "I been drip wit dis greyful poop on"—for his unreconstructed ebonics and his insistent donning of cool, foot-fungus-fighting *huaraches* on hot summer days. I still remember his milk-and dark-chocolate feet stuck in 'em. Smelled like boiled okra they did all July, all August too. Plinko! He'd gotten those sandals at a steal *thanks* to Usonia's Free-Raid Agreement with Mexico *[NAFTA?]*. ("Be grateful for the benefits of pan-capitalism," President Berzelius "Coach" Windrip admonished his Usonian constituency during his inaugural speech of 2052.)

A year later, he and a brother from the "hood" (a drug-dealing silent-partner who bank-rolled the business) opened the Smog-Cutter Lounge.

TAR SPACKLED BANNER

During "The Troubles," the neo-Fascist uprisings culminating in Texas's secession and Durfuherman's Rebellion in Idaho, Montana, Wyoming he sold out his 50% share in the biz, immigrated to Turkey, married a local woman, and joined in their desperate struggle against the Bosnian invasion of his adopted homeland. Finally got to use his West Point training. Plinko! Bozotic coincidence: both he and my son dodging Genemort attacks—a deadly gas that attacks the genes, a very painful death unless one commits suicide first—and bash-banging in the Greater Bosnian War from opposite fronts. *Moreover.* They both suicided within a day of each other after being gassed with Genemort in separate rumbles. Don left a wife and young son. My son left only me and my (now) ex-wife.

Moreover. A word I use often as both an ambiguous bridging term and an Anglo synonym for Sartre's existentialist French term, *de trop,* meaning 'being there for nothing, pure facticity'; a pingful descriptive for my historical *situatedness* within these *disunited* states of Usonia—The Bunker State. What President Ronnie Reagan observed upon returning from visiting Latin America *[Dec. 15, 1987],* he could have said about "The States" on the day of my birth, 2005: "You'd be surprised. They're all individual countries." *O.K.* I'm pessimistic. Inclined toward Calvin (rather than Calvin Klein.) Predestination. (Rather than pre-shrunk.) But I've been proven correcteroo mucho more than wrongeroo. *And then.* I'm blarghfully fated for some bozotic variety of skin canceroo *thanks* to diminishing ozone. ("Be grateful for the crosses you have to bear," my Catholic-Dad admonished me after returning from Lourdes.) I don't peep synth-beans about my physical diseaseroos, but I do absolpeep *[completely understand?]* what is psychobozotically bothering me. A life lived partially within parentheses. *But I can't treat it in my own time.* I do hotly and polymorphously perversely embraceroo the infamous 20 tenets of *Sexual Democracia* (Sex Demo), that imported spicy Latin American version of democracy in which political decisions are made according to sexual desireroo. And I put my authorial mouth where my balls are. (Isn't that what male authors o' yore did unselfconsciously? Now it takes an effort. Even the black market can't cough up any more copies of Henry Miller's novels since The Big Baneroo.) I'm even now periodically personally persecuted by The Citizens' Un-Usonian Thoughts & Activities Committee for being a jalapeño-colored condom-carrying memberoo of same. Blatantly advertised such on my webcyte by a cute animated GIF of a tiny green-condom with legs, feet clad in *huaraches,* strutting impatiently to-and-fro before the bullet-ridden Usonian White House. Copped, damnbetcha, from Sex Demo's webcyte (URL: glbo://www.sex.demo.glbo.con.dom).

Moreover. I teach "Uterineroo" (Aussie Feminism, "Criticism from Below is Aussome"), "The Pleasure of the Text: Writerly Writing," "Advanced Plagiarism." In the summer session do a Rétro-Experiences seminar in conventional typewriter production called "Lettrism and the Remington."

TAR SPACKLED BANNER

These all in the Masters in Writing Program at The Combined Art Schools of the Americas, Chicago Loop campus (C.A.S.A.-C.L.) in Chicagary, North Usonia. Blargh! My professorial slice-of-the-pie a wedge-shaped office on a too-hot-in-the-summer and too-cold-in-the-winter floor in the upper east region reserved for part-time faculty in the former State of Illinois Building (the late Helmut Jahn, architect). I light-pen mark e-mailed papers CR or NCR. Download gigabyte Master Theses files for peep and approval. Compulsively surf the "Nyet" stealing material for my classes and books. I peep out on the precariously-tilting bulk of the 125-story Meglin-Beitler Memorial Tower, the C-4 yourself handiwork of Bosnian *scarerrorists*. I try not to crank [*think*] about Sturgeon's (blarghful) Law, but my perpetually moving digital sign, the last artwork done by femino-conceptualist Jenny Holzer prior to her mysterious disappearance, silently re-recranks [*constantly reminds*] me:

CRAP... 90% OF EVERYTHING IS CRAP...90%

I'm not super superstitious. *But.* Today *is* Friday the 13th, June 2055! Exactly 1 week prior to my 50th birthday. (Or June 13th 1997 if I jump into my Maytag dryer and set the timer to 29 minutes.) So I've already treated myself to a gifteroo my ex-wife would've never gotten me: a spanking brand-nova Taco Bell Sizzlin IV-U KaPow-R-Book (*Hecho en Mexico*). Runs on a DOS EQUIS 8.6 environment, with 18 gigagulp liquid-drive, 100 megagulps of RAM, a mañana 8600 modem, only 20mm thickeroo, and features their heap nova mini-mouse. That being a tongue-driven, insert-in-the-mouth, lime sliceroo-shaped/flavored touchpad. *Let your tongue do the clickin',* runs the advert. Ever French kisseroo a computer? Much sexieroo than those passéist finger-driven deviceroos. Ya peep? *Moreover.* Pingful day to start doing *skull-time,* seeking the etiology of a diseaserooed syndrome denominated by my parents as "J.A. Ellis," seen in my Aunt Betty Baskette's eyes and in her hall mirror at 8 months, and maintained throughout my existence by TBS as such through its ideological state apparatuses and discursive regimes. [*Ellis perceives his subjectivity akin to that theorized by 20th-century psycho-analyst Jacques Lacan.*]   *   *   *

Betty Baskette's Eyes

Young Ellis's Eyes

III

Perhaps he believes that the lights will more than balance the darkness [like a well-exposed photograph] . . . seldom . . . has the autobiographer . . . been led into conscious lying about external facts. Coloring and omission are more frequent.
—Edgar Johnson, *One Mighty Torrent* (1937)

Paolo Soleri's *Arcosanti* project, near Phoenix, Arizona

Soleri's "Arcosanti" goes up in smoke (6-30-2005)

Grepping through time-lines and my baby book. Glork! Discovered I was born the very year and baptised the very day—a Baphometic Fire-baptism—the Black Stetsons, Arizona's neo-Fascist rétro-cowboy, pistol-packing separatists, bomberooed Italian architect Paolo Soleri's utopian Arcosanti 2000 architectural project near Phoenix, Arizona. Just completed after years of slow, ill-financed construction, the famous **architecture + ecology = arcology** experiment was heap devastated. Blargh! Never did get a peep by acquaintance, only by description later. *[Hierarchies of knowledge, respectively rooted in presence and absence, theorized by philosopher Bertrand Russell and which French theorist Jacques Derrida's Deconstructionism discredited by claiming that: "There is nothing outside the text."]* Only signs—images in books and webcytes—never the referent. Arcosanti now only exists in hyper-reality *[as a simulacrum]*. Ya peep?

8

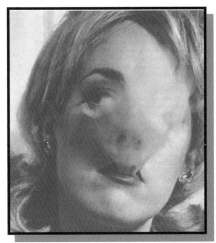

Mother 6 months prior to my birth

Dad upon first seeing me

Smokeroo. Boo-hoo! It heap pervades my life. Mother was—ugh, bletch!—a chain-smoker. Father too. Proof the late-1990s ban on tobacco adverts had not mucho neg-effect on my parents' generation. Here they are as photographed by each other. Turned each other into images. Dead—they are now at once metaphoric substitutions, illusions of presence and by that same token, metonyms, signs of their absence and my loss. But am I any different? Here's a scan of a digi-pic made of me in my faculty "wedge" the day I started teaching at C.A.S.A.-C.L. It ran in the September 2035 issue of the

J.A. Ellis (2035) posed "candid" portrait for school paper; note the rétro-Remington typewriter sitting in the background

school's newspaper *F___ed Up* for the purposes of identification. As an *image* it marks the site of an ambivalence. It makes *pres-ent* something that is *absent*— and temporarily deferred—it is the representation of a time that is always elsewhere. Now that I do crank *[think]* of it, not unlike my displacing time in the madly spinning Maytag. In a way, I'm neither *here* nor *there.* It's never the simple case of an "appear-ance" of a "reality." The access to the image of my identity is only ever possible in the *negation* of any sense of originality or plenitude, ya peep?

TAR SPACKLED BANNER

Smoke and mirrors! The story of my formative years. Maybe why I always had digi-scaneroos and paintings covering my childhood bedroom—and still do today. Glork! Curious how this blarghful painting of Mt.

Mt. Machhapuchhare ht. 7,059 mt.

Machhapuchhare (ht. 7,059 meters) was, since time T equals minus infinity *[a long time ago]*, my heap fav. I bubble *[recall]* that, besides the odd name of this mountain (it also is called "The Fishtail"), I was drawn to the wonky red grass under the tree on the right. (Why I later was drawn to Fauvist paintings?) I've never peeped this Himalayan scene "in reality," but imagined it to be pigmental embodiment of the pingful and mysterious Mount Analogue in René Daumal's unfinished Surrealist novel of the same name. A text *[first published in 1952]* that promised to eager young peepers: "A Novel of Symbolically Non-Euclidean Adventures in Mountain Climbing." How could the kid resist? Prodigious peeper, even when heap youngeroo, I memed *[memorized]* Daumal's bozotic jingle and rap-sung it over and over mucho to Mom's chagrin. My mirror to her smoke. Ya peep?

The Lay of the Luckless Mountaineers

> *The tea tastes of aluminum;*
> *12 sleeping-bags for 30 men—*
> *Everyone snug as a smothered bug.*
> *Then off before the cracking dawn,*
> *Breathing air like razor blades,*
> *Between deathly black and deathly white.*

10

TAR SPACKLED BANNER

My watch had the sense to stop;
Yours has gone on a spree.
We're smeared to the elbows with honey;
The sky's all curds and whey.
It's light before we get going,
The névé's already turned yellow,
It's already raining pebbles,
And the cold seeps into your hands.
Who put gasoline in the drinking water?
Our fingers swell like sponges,
And the rope feels like a telegraph pole.
The shelter's jumping with fleas;
Our snoring sounds like the Paris zoo.
My ear's cracking off from frostbite.
You look like a half-trussed duck. . . .

I forget the rest 'cept for stanza pertaining to memory and representation:

This rock ledge won't give up.
You know what I have? A memory block,
A stomach cramp, a flaming thirst,
And 2 fingers turned pale green.
We never did see the summit—
Except on the sardine can. . . .

Years later, I did peep a scene heap sim to this suggestive painting. From a hot-air balloon. A *real* vista. Mt. Glitterntin in Arboretum's famous mountain range dubbed "Da Catkins" by those eco-botanized offshoots of Charles Forester and his Bloody Brigade of Secessionist-Slaughterers. *And then.* Later, as an acanemic, I realized Daumal and I had mucho in common—a rarity even between Usitizens today. We both struggled—he because he was a poet, I because I was a product of the fabled "Linguistic Turn" in philosophy—with the tendency to conceive of life and reality entirely through language.

From this fascination with heights, I dove down, down. A precocious child raised on Globo-Com's re-reruns of *Sea Hunt* wanted to fathom the depths. But chronic sinuhurtus made even a fathom-under blarghful torture. *And then.* Scuba sublimated into spelunking, exploring caves. Until blarghful discovery of claustrophobia. Further sublimation: *Reading about* scuba and spelunking on Usenets. Later, deeper: alt.phil.plato.cave, downloading huge bytes of Freud's *Interpretation of Dreams* and Jung's *Man and his Symbols,* finally finding through Lacan LANGUAGE at the bottom of everything. Any wonder I studied Down Under? Degree in Uterineroo from www.monash. edu.au.

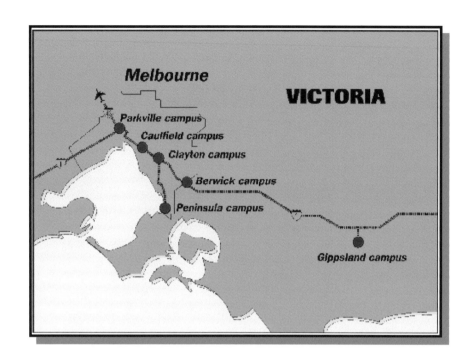

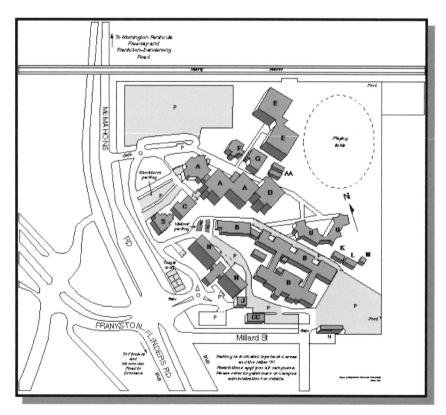

TAR SPACKLED BANNER

Did all grad E-mailrespondence coursework with Monash University via the Net. "Mon Ass," as the wits call it, was founded in the elder-days to extend the ops for a coll.edu to the urbanasses *[urban masses]*. *And then.* Virtual diploma—*Magna Cum Laude*—offered in quicky download of 100 megabytes. But even then curiosity and ping of travel calls. Flew Quantas's "Sizzling Barbie" supersonic jetliner to Melbourne, hailed a nova Automatty Cab and after several minutes of confusion on setting the controls, went to Monash's

I receive my diploma and a handshake from the Dean

My departmental chairman

Peninsula Campus (see maps on preceding page) to feel a real parched hand hand me the parchment. Came home with images of my success. Ready to commit error-33, predicating 1 research effort, a nova hypertextual Uterineroo webcyte I hoped would land me a post in acanemia, upon the success of another, my 2.3 gigabyte dissertation. Amused my folks with after-dinner stories about the gumby *[a stupid bureaucrat]* from the Dean's Office, Klaus, who took me to The Alumni Barbie serving up insanely great Chernobyl Chicken *[Lemon Chicken]* on tables under a grove of old Wolleni pine. I *did not* tell them about Hildie.

While in Melbourne, I encouraged a flirtatious come on to come out back and get down under the Southern Cross for a humpdayboinkeroo by that gumby's wife, served up *à la* tipsieroo, by explaining to her the crux of my dissertation: "To this day, nearly 50 years post elder-days, it is required in acanemia that the level of reflection be a high one (like Mt. Machhapuchhare), the level of theory higher still (like Mt. Analogue); the drop to lower levels of feeling and concretizations (spelunking in Plato's Cave, scubadiving in Mallarmé's Swan's lake) is considered precipitious and sub-genius. But asks Uterineroo, that Aussome Fem Theory, is there any such thing as the *height of theory*, except as an element in matty masculinist mystique?"

TAR SPACKLED BANNER

Baffled, Hildie responded with her own semiotics, poking her right index finger through a hole formed—ho!—by curling together her left index finger and thumb, pumping it slowly back and forth. An hour later she was mixing us both very strong O.J. Bronco's in a negligible negligée. She wore a UL-Approved UV-repellant silver wig. I still see her every time I quaff an O.J.

Hildie ever on my mind

In gratitude for my acanemic persistence and my postprandial *histoire obligatoire*, Father bought me a briar pipe to match my nova Taco-Bell Armani grey tweed, leather elbow-patched sports coat. Mother bought me a real authentic replica of a rétro-knock-off of a Streamline Moderne 24-karat gold cigarette case. Both useful in an image-mindful acanemia, they thought. Never used 'em though. They sit today as ever-bubbles *[reminders]* of my deceased parents on my synthoak laminate mantelpiece in my bullet-ridden Chicagary flat in Lincoln Square. N'er did I e'er puff. Didn't have to, the nation's been up in smoke since my birth. Smog and the acrid smell of cordite. The moderately obscure attitude adopted by the Left—*Fascism can never triumph since we are mucho more clever*—was proven to be pure political fritterware by the violent events of the post elder-days. We peeped something bad-wonky when McDonald's, in a last-ditch attempt to fight Taco Bell take-overs, offered an increasingly impoverished and violent constituency their heap cheap $9.95 special, the

A conspirator hangs

McVeigh Sup-R-Value-Pak (flaming dog-food patty on an open bun, scorched chicken fingers, burnt fries, and a Bloody Mary). Released on the very day that Fasci-hero bomber was finally executed *by hanging*. Glork, if he didn't win a Usonian Supreme Court decision from those 80-column juridical minds permitting him to exit this vale of political fears pants-shitting and feet-kicking like the Lincoln Conspirators in those roust-about Reb rebellious glory days of yore. Globo-Com teled it globally via satellite through their Ascension Island studio stronghold. A gay yak—the famous Aussie quizz-game host for "Let's Make a Steal"—lisped: "Thay mates—I just can't, Mic, convey thay eeeemotion surroundang thay execution of thas con, McVeigh, tawday." *Soon thereafter.* Barbershops in South Usonia featured the "McVeigh-Cut." *Playgirl* did a double-page spread the following month of McVeigh's nude corpse on a gurney, caption reading: "Well-hungeroo."

Those symbols of TBS's social order so prominent during such national events—the spandex-clad police, the bugle calls, military parades and waving flags, free tranquilex fudge, and those black helicopters overhead—are both heap inhibitory and heap stimulating. They want to convey the blarghful message "Don't dare budgeroo," but rather they pingfully cry out "Get ready to attackeroo!" The next question is: Who attackerooed? Plinko! It wasn't the Left, pilgrim! They'd pulled a neo-liberal gumby *[stupid fuckup]* and voluntarily turnerooed in their firepower (even air- and squirt-guns) to their local police stations during The Great Disarmament campaign of 2001. Now they got hosed.

Culti-multuralism (cultural, racial harmony) died a violent death within the sights of the M&Ms (maniacal monoculturalists). Amigoization was replaced by the tight nooses of the "White Cap" vigilantes who lynched Mexican migrant workers, *los hanging chickens,* in what was soon the independent Nova Republik of Texas (announced by an outrageous flag, see frontispiece). These "White Caps," in a self-conscious remake of Hollywood's anti-Mexican film *The Professionals,* even had the *generosidad* to invade 175 miles south of the Tex-Mex border to bid a violent *buenas noches* to the Skinnerian utopists and autistic children housed at the famous Behaviorist *Comunidad Los Horcones.* In Idaho and Montana, fasci-agitator, Mark Durfuherman, advocated laws closing all ethnic food restaurants. (It was blarghfully rumored, but never proven, that his movement was backed-up by secret big-number funds from McDonald's since such legislation could be used to shut down all competing Taco Bell food concessions.) Vari-responses from the Left to this *othercide* were:

■ Ethno-feminists, NAFTA art dealers, and Border Brujo's pray fervently to Santa Frida Kahlo.

A Border Brujo prays

TAR SPACKLED BANNER

■ The septuagenarian Marxist critic Benjamin H.D. Buchloch citing an earlier Marxist cranker *[thinker]*, Walter Benjamin: *The state of emergency in which we live is not the exception but the rule. We must attain to a concept of history that is in keeping with this insight.*

■ Mass migrations to Denmark, Sweden, Finland, Holland, Australia, New Zealand, Tasmania, El Salvador, Costa Rica, Argentina, Nicaragua, and Colombia. Usonian expatriates happily singing nova national anthems—like Colombia's stirring *Oh, gloria inmarcesible! Oh, jubilo inmortal!*

■ Ritual mass suicides make Jim Jones and the other culticides seem small potatoes. The largest single exit, some 2000 souls, is the result of arsenic-laced Laser Chicken *[Kung Pao Chicken]* freely passed around in San Francisco Metroland Bay Area's famous Chinatown district during the Chinese New Year celebrations.

■ Hispanics less pessimistic. Firmer belief in *mañana!* The virtual barrio, La Chicano Interneta, is born. Vatoman (a Chicano Batman), El Naftazteca, and Supermojado, a border hero, come on-line to promote *gringostroika* (the overthrow "by any means" of pan-capitalism and its replacement by Aztlán) as well to agit-prop against the harsh policies and all-elbows enforcement of what they call *Miki Mikiztli Califas* (Náhuatl for "California, the house of death").

■ At the peak of "The Troubles," a *ménage-à-contre-troubles* of wonky Leftists formed, under General Charles Cane Forester, The North Usonia Loyalist Alliance Freedom Brigade. They put down the bloody Durfuherman Rebellion and founded Arboretum to boot. (Rumor has it Taco Bell money financed the Brigade for the soldiers' food-ration was high in beans and tortillas.)

*   *   *

PART TWO

I

*. . . there are only four occupations worthy of a man: actor, rock
star, jet fighter pilot, or President of the United States.*
—emblazoned on the press book of the film *Top Gun* (1986)

*Our replacements will be vastly superior to ourselves as image
actualizers: they will be built for anamorphosis. Welcome to the
post-God era.*
—Arthur Kroker and Michael Weinstein, *Data Trash* (1994)

Post Christian body spasmeroo. I couldn't tolerate unbearable tension of
divided experience. By the time I reached the age of reason I was a
fully-wired incept *[Kroker/Weinstein's term for a body oriented toward
the media-net]*, sliderooing ecstatically into Globo-Comic virtuality. Seeing
is HDTV, hearing is Globo-MTVIII, sniffing is coke, puffing is smoke, cranking
[thinking] is Taco Bell DOS EQUIS wetware. Ya peep? Only required to
digitally snore on the virtual Sabbath, Kranch-Day, doing penance for our
cynical anamorphosis *[the perverted image of virtual reality]*. I'd display the
required Globo-emoticon signifying *Sorry, kranching* on my webcyte and e-
mail transponder so all'd peep my enforced digi-sleep:

TAR SPACKLED BANNER

An inneroo reality of soft parasiteroo began to grow unrelieved, enhanced even, by the kranching. Fact: TBS mega-brainly peeped that weekly plug-downs revs up inneroo need for mega-inception. On the *recline.* Strategy of declining life, weakening life needing more electro-prosthetics. The will to virtuality. *Go to primary document*—Thus Spake Ellis—*to confirm.* Bytes from my 4-U Taco-Bell Hallmark Diary-Entry 4.3 fritterware—which features Signa-Catch Baptismal Font that generateroos a font of your own handwritting after scannerooing a hard-copy page of your personal scribble—from age 11:

D.E.: 11-09-2016—

I only have pingfun when I'm jacked-in. I'm more relaxeroo, more sociable and wonky too. I don't crank about what I peep like to others. I even bust-bubble to go to the bathroom or playeroo with my choad. Kranching only puts bletchful nausea back into my wakes and dreams, but it does heap serve its purps: making you automagically appreciate the pings of virtual things. Insanely great ideroo.

I made a sketcheroo about what it felt like to re-incept after 24 hours of kranching—euphoria of body loss. *Like being an angel,* I cranked. A 1000 points of coherent light. A sensationeroo milked for mega-bucks by the infamous Neo-Catholic webholycyte incepted at Nova Rome, South Usonia and gloriously globally accessed via the URL: globo://et.com.spiri/220). Nova Rome was rumorooed to have twice as mucho virtual unreal estate as old Rome had real. It's heap mucho pop download for web-whackers was the virtual "Stations of the Cross" in which, to cite the cyte's ad-blurberoo, "The guarderoos

Angel of the Incept (2016)

18

The First Station of the Cross

hardprod as Christ 'trodes the circuit to Getsomeinformee." At each Station, a surpriseroo nova webcyte is heap pusherooed onto your browser and you find yourself surfing off shores unwanted and un-peeped. *Like being heap pre-destined.* Station #4 might send you to the web-adcyte touting a "Hologram-O-Christ, a virtual comfort for display virtually any place, bunker-mantel or armored car dashboard." Station #1 might find you witnesseroo to "The Virtualous Nun, Sr. Soguk Dudak" giving a pious *apologia* for both the TBS's *and* its adversaries' all-elbows approach to social relations; she calls for heap patience and forgiveness via a creepingly elegant Christian commentary upon St. Hanlon's Razor—an inspired blurb written in prison in 2005, just prior to this young hacker-nun's (Sister Merge Hanlon) electrocution at the 'trode-stake in Old Rome for femino-heresy:

Never attribute to malice that which can be adequately explained by stupidity.

—St. Hanlon

Station #8 explained Apostolic Succession as "a Play of the Papal Signifier" in which Pope Virtual I was touted as the legitimate nova line of Popes residing in Nova Rome. The last Station predestined you to suffer a flashing, animated GIF of discorporate Pope Virtual I cyber-blessing you while he hacked into your system, putting across your screen or VR-goggles or (if you're a 'trode, in your mind) the endless Virtual Revivalist message urging the unjacked-in to:

FIX. . . GET HOOKED ON THE CRUCIFIX, THE ULTIMATE FIX. . . GET

19

You played helleroo trying to exorcise this Virtuous Virus. Besides, the Stations, another pop branch off the main cyte was the "Hailicous Mary" in which you were hailed by a "Virtual Mary, full of 'trodes" to Globo-glomonto *[purchase via the web]* "a maryid" of prayerful prods *[products],"* such as the comforting *Hörauftriebuch [audioupliftbook]* for the "double-troubled debteroo-ridden": *Dying of Consumption? Insightful Commentary on the Consumer's Bible, Chapter 11,* or the heap pop downloadable hypertexteroo *Shop 'Til You Drop Yet Redeem Yourself and Your Coupons.* Ya peep?

Hacking the soul is how media-analysts peeped this nova phenomenon of directed advertising. *A direct reverseroo of elder-day hacking,* explained De Puté McLoohan in his pop heap-seller, *Push 'n Shrive: The Virtue of Virtual Ministries* (2009), that analyzed the blarghfulness of such pushy-push-cytes—a web-tactic also used with agit-prop effect by the M&Ms (those manical monoculturalists we love to hate). He appealed to all Net Useroos: *Freedom is no longer even virtual. Freedom's become officialdumb. Hackeroos unite!*

Of course, *uniting* was the crux of the issue as disparate thingeroos tore at the social tissue of Usonia like piranha. A chewy *[tough]* problemeroo in a modemist socius where *ex*-centric, *dis*-integrated, *dis*-located, *dis*-juncted, *dis*-corporate, de-construction, *dis*-continuous, *dis*-associated, and *de*-regulated are the heap all-muscled *[dominant]* prefixes; where mass gatherings have been, courtesy of TBS, *Verboten* since the onset of The Troubles.

Moreover. Function, form, and meaning have ceaserooed to have any relationship to each other. In architecture, a quonset hut facade is the entrance to a mega-buck residence; a mega-buck residence hides an ammo-dump; a Brooks Brothers suit cloaks the fasci-hard heart of an AmPat cadre; the honorable accolades of Senatorial office hide a former foolish, even venomous, Yak *[talk-show host]* lurking within. The infamous *Chicanagary Rebelde Virtual Barrio* (CRVB) webcyte—their sexual democracia-spun editorial slogan is *Poner en evidencia* ("To reveal")—lists *Los Malcalidade*s (The Badqualities) contributing to the *Weltschmerz* of the modemist badcondition of *Desmodernidad* (my translation):

CRVB ¡PONER EN EVIDENCIA!

LIFE: A JUMBLE OF FRAMES AND SEQUENCES, LAP DISSOLVES, FADE-INS AND FADE-OUTS, JUMP-CUTS.

TAR SPACKLED BANNER

THE COSMOS: A JUMBLE OF VIOLENT ACCIDENTS, A DISCONTINUOUS STRUCTURE OF POINTS.

RULING PARADIGM: THE ACCIDENT OF THE EXPLOSION IS THE NORM. THE ONLY CERTAINTY: THE PUNCTUM, THE POINT, THE POINT OF DETONATION.

We once peeped a heap unified world—like that in "Leave it to Beaver" on 1950s TV. (But even then crack in totality hinted at whenever Mrs. Cleaver said: "Ward, I think something's wrong with the Beaver.") *And then.* Later could only peep phantom organ of totality—like re-runs of that TV show. *But now*, in our state of *recline*. Can only *desire* to peep phantom organ of such totality—like the several big-screen remakes of that TV show starting back in 1997. This is the core of my thesis in *Data Trash Recycled* (*DTR*), my scholarly study of Kroker/Weinstein's post elder-days classic analysis of early pan-capitalism, cultural re-cline and recombinant fasc-ism. Two divergent exempla of such *desire for totality* at 2 different cultural levels as culled from chapter 1 of my text:

Don-de-bartender (upper right) caught on Globo-Com coverage (7-4-2035)

Genemort gas attack (known among the troops as 'Mendel 's Revenge'), Turko-Bosnian Front (2028), digi-photo found in cam-mem on dead Divided Nations Trooper

    I. Acanemic: Martin Heidegger's 'listening for Being.'
    II. Globo-pop: listening to vintage Roy Orbison vinyls (DTR, 9).

Losing battleroo: try to crank [*think*] this without feeling nostalgia! Resultant: *retread* culture. Retreaded as often as Don-de-bartender's *huaraches* had been resoled—he'd been on several Million Man mar-ches on Washington. His wid-ow had sent those sandals—he called 'em his "scandals"—to me, along with

**Don's grave slab (foreground)
Erdine, Turkey (anon. digi-pic)**

a photograph shot off the televison by his mother, as a virtual memento of her poor Genemort-gassed hubby's heap strong anti-M&M, pro-sexual democracia political belief-eroos. He had patriotically answered The Voice of Turkey's desperate, but clever, broadcast plea for volunteers from foreigners residing within her borders—*Be Here There!* —then Turkey's northwestern border was attacked and overrun by ethnic-cleansing Bosnian scaretroops. That dark, deadly gas attack had so blarghfully jumbled his jolly genes that even Clone-Grown's Sav-Cloning procedures wouldn't have been able to salvage him. May he recline in heap peace in his stone slab grave near Edirne, Turkey not far from where he was fatally gassed. Blargh! But part of me won't remain resigned to his horrible fate. My nights are filled with unpingful visions of both Don's and my son's gassed and gasping corpses. So I'm currently trying to return to the day before, respectively, of my son's and Don's demise to warn them of their impending doom. But this means rewinding to my present time (your future),

Frontispiece, *The Life and Death of Cormac the Scald* (2009)

winding back in my crude clothes dryer *cum* time-machine. Six dizzying attempts, yet miss the date, tumble-drying into a time either heap late or, like now, heap early. Now suffer chronic vertigo. *And*, I crank some guys stalking me—TBS's terrible tumbling Tempokops. Their 80-column minds take dim view of heap time-tamperoo, saying pulling such a gumby would bogotify *[disorganize, make bogus]* the Now. One micro-event changeroo would, they say, create sagans *[billions and billions]* of tempo-slack *[temporal internal fragmentation]* in the their present and future. Fear really be that Don, spared his blarghful fate, would become an even mucho-rad politicritter. Come back to TBS to rallieroo his mucho put-upon-People against the slam-shutters *[closed minds]* of the M&Ms. He might even take on that horrible Black-boiling rétro-Norseman fasci-critter known as "Cormac the Scald" whose blarghful boiling exploits against people of color and bozotic rétro-garb (he claimed Icelandic heritage and was an autodidactical expert on Medieval Icelandic Sagas) are dastardly detailed in Snorre Sturlason's favorable biography, *The Life and Death of Cormac the Scald* (Vidor, Nova Republik of Texas: AmPat Dissident Press, 2009); therein, Sturlason claims Cormac started his glorious career as the famous (or infamous, depending on your politics) Corrections officer at the Pelican Bay SHU (Security Housing Unit) in the San Franciso Bay area who was summarily dismissed in the mid-1990s for forcibly scalding a black inmate in a hot-water bath. He later resurfaces in Vidor, Texas *[a notorious KKK-dominated town]* just prior to that state's secession and convinces local KKK members to burn their white

The Galloping Galahad Patch designed by Cormac the Scald

sheets, don helmets and chain-mail, and abjure the lynching bee in favor of holy war with sword and boiling water. He gatherooed nova recruits by attending meetings of The Society for Creative Anachronism, infecting those impressionable medieval *poseurs* with their evil doctrine. Claiming: "We'll be da ruin yet o' thems apes 'n mongrels!" he advertised his helmeted warriors via a nova fasci-logo based on ancient runes; its macho design was tagged "The Galloping Galahad," later bogotified by pop yak into "Da Gallopin' Gal I Had." Besides his graphic skills, Cormac attained some notoriety for his "gangsta art," some of which were reproduced in a portfolio section in Sturlason's bozotic biography.

A Cut Above (colored pencil, 2004)
Collection of Rush Limbugh Jr.

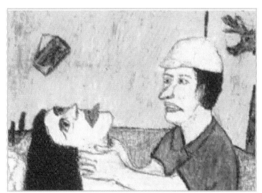

No More Mañanas (colored pencil, 2005)
Collection of Fort Worth Art Museum

PORTFOLIO: CORMAC THE SCALD

Upstairs/Downstairs (ink on school notebook paper, 1985)
Cormac's early (teenage) style (Fort Worth Art Museum)

Cormac, wearing helmet and holding a sprig of scrub-brush, took to the soap-box in defenseroo of the Starchies' *[white supremacists]* infamous "Will to Purity Program," pop-peeped as "Da Big Scrub," advocating (*Ach du Scheiß!*):

𝔢𝔱𝔥𝔫𝔦𝔠 𝔠𝔩𝔢𝔞𝔫𝔰𝔦𝔫𝔤

𝔯𝔞𝔠𝔦𝔞𝔩 𝔠𝔩𝔢𝔞𝔫𝔰𝔦𝔫𝔤

𝔰𝔢𝔵𝔲𝔞𝔩 𝔠𝔩𝔢𝔞𝔫𝔰𝔦𝔫𝔤

𝔦𝔫𝔱𝔢𝔩𝔩𝔢𝔠𝔱𝔲𝔞𝔩 𝔠𝔩𝔢𝔞𝔫𝔰𝔦𝔫𝔤

But stopped short of touting Globo-Com Net cleansing; supposedly, he'd been paid off by nervous executives with a cost-free webcyte to advertise his Starchy shenanigans. This blarghful bit of backsliding cost him his liferoo.

TAR SPACKLED BANNER

Mark Durfuherman (front) as a young Skinhead in New Jersey

Cormac's anti-Semitic poster advertising the power of using Globo-Com Net for Far Right Agit-Prop; it was denounced by Durfuherman's Fasci-Group as being idealistic and pacificistic

Arriving for a clandestine strategy meeting with the Montana fascist Mark Durfuherman, he was embraced so warmly and evil-energetically by his stout host that, despite his chain-mail, Cormac's ribcage was horribly crusherooed. Durfuherman, a strict cyber-Luddite, was incensed by a recent poster Cormac's group had issued (see illustration). His very last agonized words, gasped through bloody blood, were said to have been: "Dishonored I die." To which Durfuherman was said to have replied: "Oh short, oh short then be thy reign, 'n give us the world again." Internment—his mangled corpse accompanied by his sword and recipe for Boil'd Black Puddin'—was in Fort Davis, Nova Republik of Texas near the Davis Observatory in the Fort Davis Mountains whose *astronomers* were "butcher'd 'n boil'd 'n skinn'd" by Cormac's band of raiding rétro-Norsemen and replaced by *astrologers*. The usual headstone inscription:

R.I.P.

was appropriately changed to:

D.I.D.

to commemorate Cormac's last words.

[*Obviously, Cormac was fully aware that there actually is an Icelandic saga known as* The Life and Death of Cormac the Skald *or* Kormak's Saga *which was written sometime between 1250 - 1300 A.D. by an unknown author and translated into English by W.G. Collingwood and J. Stefansson (Ulverson, 1901); for further information download the following website:*

http://www.anglia.co.uk/angmulti/vikings/saga/about.html.]

TAR SPACKLED BANNER

Cormac the Scald's Globo-Com webcyte logo

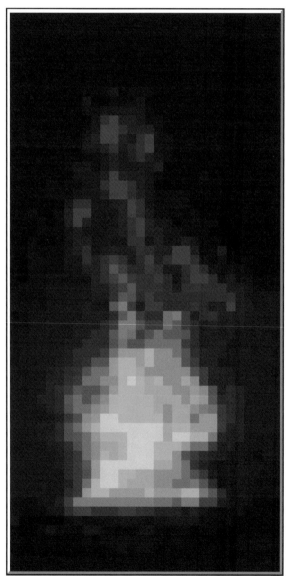

The Digital Holocaust (2007) Cormac's first
attempt at computer art as run on his webcyte

Surfascist Victory Communique No.2:

Comrades! Girlfriends! We trimuphantly announce the first report on a corpse having no body— America has vanished!

In Art, we appreciate humor that can't take a joke.

Evisceration will give the middle-classes the emptiness they crave.

Incineration is sublime! Let them speak of rights as they inhale the flames.

We are Surfacists! We will fulfill everyone's needs!

TAR SPACKLED BANNER

Cormac's *Surfacists* webcyte initiated a variety of cyber-responserooes. When in Australia, I culled from the University of Monash's archives an editorial cartooneroo that had run in the *Sydney Times Right-Now*, a right-wing news-

"Cormac tops a Commie at Usonia's Leftist Democratic Party Headquarters"
by Nev Quinn in "Editorials," *Sydney Times Right-Now* **(Aug. 21, 2006)**

paper. Interestingly, the same cartooneroo ran simultaneously in the weekly tabloid *Socialism Now*, but was captioned: "Fasci-violence breaks out at Usonia's Democratic Party Headquarters." The vital strategy used here—doubling-coding—had already been in use by the 1990s, but was perfected by Globo-Com. This cartoonist from Down-Under cleverly tuned the 'tune to go pingfully *[pleasantly well]* with either the Goosestep or the Soupy Shuffle *[a shuffling dance movement invented by TV comic Soupy Sales in the 1960s; has it become rétro-stylish among liberals by the early 21st century?]*. Context and the peeper's politi-peeps mucho determine whether one decodes it as lampooning Cormac or identifying with his anti-Left violence. And there's always the 5% who can't decideroo *which* peep *[interpretation]* is correct and another 5% in "spasm" *[Kroker-Weinstein's term for a state of living with absolutely contradictory feeling all the time]* who feel *both* peeps are correct. The pingfulness *[beautiful elegance]* of it is that *both* Rightist and Leftist will have their peep-systems re-enforcerooed by the *same* imageroo. Ho! Saves time and money. Foments blarghful antagonism between and within groups. Makes it easier *to divide and conquer.* Promotes the formation of SSPC (small-scale private crazies) at the expense of large, well-organized groups. TBS's typical strategy for containment and neutralizeroo—ya peep? *[The Bunker State's officials must be up on their Foucault and Baudrillard, sensing the benefit of these thinkers' "elder-day" post-liberal ideas to unwittingly do the "fasci-flip-flop" in favor of generating even more intensified and penetrating capillary methods of social control. Did (would) the postmodernists' attack on the heroic individual simply, on the one hand, re-enforce TBS's ability to reproduce docile social subjects, and on the other, promote a pseudo-heroicism attained via violent Fascist action groups, such as the Skinheads and Cormac's band of merry scalders and hackers (on-line and with a sword)?]*

Plinko! We have liverooed for 2500 years with what James Joyce called "ABCED-mindedness" until the advent of the telematic tribal world of Post-literate Man in the elder-days *[yet this concept was first identified by Marshall McLuhan in the late 1950s]*. Damnbetcha, switcherooed from linear to cluster configurations of info. By the era of Generation-X, literate society was dying and providing heap less motivation for the teaching of reading and the achieving of literate culture. A diminution of interest in all previous achievement, except for a fascination with past episodes of racial/ethnic cleansing. Difference between education and entertainment erased by 2000 A.D. when domestic terrorists destroy the old capital dome and TBS builds its Nova White House in the shape of a Celtic Cross next to the Pentagon.

Floor Plan of the Nova White House, Usonia

Books and blackboards replaced by the fun of skinny-dipping by electronic flesh. Now everything happens to everyone at the same time. *Simultaneity of the global village* is how Marshall McLuhan saw it. Tribal juxtaposition. Archipelagoes of disparate language games. *Boycott the exceptional!* became the generational rallying cry of The Class of 2005 A.D. The tribe: a social-seeking of mediocrity as a means of achieverooing Mateyness *[together-ness]*. White-power tribes on the short-wave. White-power tribes on Globo-Com Net. But Virtual White-power has heap nostalgia for the maimed body. Generation-Xers attainerooed this by body piercings. But Generation-XX wants more than labrets and simulation, needs *real* versions of those heap pop virtual-reality games "V-Storm-Trooper" and "Virtual Reich 2000." Each generation sets patterns of painful experiencerooes that must be accepted (in chronological order):

Depression Era: empty stomachs and lynching
Baby-Boomers: spanking and slapping the face
Generation-X: hard-drive crashing and body-piercing
Generation-XX: kranching and scalding
Generation-XXX: spasm and homelessness

TAR SPACKLED BANNER

Ho! You. Wake up! Yes, you, heap Peeper! Dogged, uninsultable, video-oriented bastard, it's you I'm addressing! Who else *[play on "Ellis"?]*, from inside this monstrous (check 1 or both):

□**Fiction**　　□**Documentary**

Caught you dozing off. Or—blargh!—maybe you're just 1 of those 80-column minds who not peeperoo this stuff mucho. What you say? I often speak in the first person, tiresome? Well . . . each to his or her opinion. *And then.* Who—when every subatomic interaction consists of the annihilation of the original particles and the creation of new subatomic particles, a continual dance of creation and annihilation creating a never-ending, forever nova reality—am I? *Just a mindstream,* you crank? But, you who listen to me give me heap temp nova life—and *not* just in a manner of speaking. *Ergo,* I *will* hold you responsible for attenderooing to my auto-tale, just as I hold my parents responsible for conceiving *moi*, albeit, they say I don't at all resemble now what came out then from my mother's womb. But, hey dad, here I am: your *caricreature*! Ya peep?

Children are vengeance, saith Blessed John Barth, Bozotic Lord of PoMo fictioneroo and the only elder-day author to have been praised by Sogyal Rinpoche II with "having the X-Nature." *[In fact, this whole section is an X-ceptional travesty of the opening pages to John Barth's "Autobiography: A Self-Recorded Fiction" in* Lost in the Funhouse, *1968.]* Fact: My drinking pardner, "Freedom" (*Eleftheria* in Greek) Trumpoulos (you remember him from bottom of page 4?), *did* (insanely great!) sue his parents for his blargh-big Jewish-Greek nose, his "Cyranose" as he wittily dubbed it. Shades of O.J.—he won his case! His parents where judged liable for not *tonking* (a pre-natal genetic tampering procedure popularized by geneticist Henry Tonks) so his nose would fit The Great Norm (TGN). His parents were forced to pay for a conventional surgical nose- and mouth-job. For men, TGN was based on a youthful rétro-star Paul Newman's physiognomy; for women, it was based on an re-rétro

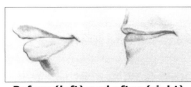

Before (left) and after (right) sketches of "Freedom's" lips

[ancient?] woodcut recently discovered depicting the legendary Helga, Iceland's Loveliest Lady. (Helga was a tragic heroine, and possibly a real person, featured in the 11th-century saga *Gunnlaugs Saga Ormstungu*, translated by William Morris and published in 1869 as *The Saga of Gunnlaug Worm [or Serpent]-tongue*).

TAR SPACKLED BANNER

Ho! What a pingfuljoe was "Freedom." When he died he was a big man with a limp, red nose, rimless glasses, big belly, dirty complexion, pudgy hands, rheumy eyes, not mucho hair. But in his post mouth- and nose-job early adulthood, he was handsome. And modest too. Complainerooed to his

**"Freedom" Trumpoulos
as a young man (2027)**

shrink he was only "moderately obscure," i.e., someone who could be figured out but probably isn't worth the trouble. And this in the heyday of West Coast Gen-XX ego-building clinics no lesseroo! Got his moniker "Freedom" for his indefatigable defense of E-zine rights against the prevailing cries for extreme censorship and tough copyright control from the infamous Suburbanite Coalition: 1) the right to publish Leftist reviews; 2) the right to capture (scan from magazines or nab from Globo-Com Net) imagery to accompany these reviews without paying the exorbitant copyright fees; 3) the right to display semi-nudity and/or make explicit reference to the sex organs *but only if the purpose was specifically for aesthetic or scholarly reasons.*

He covered his aberrant political ass by always operating this blatantly anti-pan-capitalist, pro-utopist E-zine, *Net Yet*, under the pirated unGreekful pseudonym **William Charles Kile**. His cottage publishing venture was, however, blarghfully exterminated by Usonia C.I.A. after he ran an editorial describing the vision of life in The Bunker State as:

> . . . *akin to 2 homeless children clasping dirty hands in a dead city, loud with the lethargic tedium of old apes and the heavy flight of loose-boweled peacocks, those monsters of the abyss which the psychoanalyst fishes for with nets, which the politician seeks with favors, and the general uncovers with dynamite.*

**The forged Social Security Card used by
"Freedom" Trumpoulos to avoid prosecution**

TAR SPACKLED BANNER

Always the cultural scavenger, "Freedom's" own den (he called it his "pirate's wardroom") sported an Indian miniature from the Rajput Hills that jostled an Azande *shongo,* or throwing knife, on the wall next to a Dutch painting by a minor historical talent; the den's shelves were bozotically shared by group of Australian *churingas* (a gifteroo I'd given him upon returning from my graduation at Monash U.), a plastic ultrarétroplica of a real terracotta ithyphallic *Silenos* from ancient Thebes, an authentic copy of an Iroquois turtle rattle, a diverse gaggle of Japanese *netsukes,* a Gaboon ship harp, a superb reproduction of a Corsican vendetta knife, a real Malay *kris*, and an old dueling pistol (its twin forever absent) that supposedly once belonged to an English count propped up next to the Doubleday & Co. 1953 edition of André Malraux's *The Voices of Silence* inherited from his father, Efthemios. From the latter he'd taken Malraux's dictum "All art is a revolt against man's fate," and heap Marximodifierooed it into an subjunctive epigraph for the masthead of his utopic E-zine:

Always the Habermasian-optimiest *[Jürgen Habermas, late-twentieth-century defender of Enlightenment reason, the public sphere, modernity, etc.]*, in his first editorial "Freedom" asserted:

> *Ho! Pingfully I hold that civilization—what's left of it after TBS's raj and Brahman have staggerooed forward and fallen—will move in a desirable direction; knowledge will advance, and with that advance, reason and decency must increasingly prevail among all. And Chess will be replaced by Go as the intellectual's gameroo of preference. Ya peep?*

This was on-line at a time when legions of fasci-pilgrims still sojourned south in armored cars and armed "technicals" to desolate Fort Davis, Nova Republik of Texas to pay their fasci-respects at Cormac-the-Scald's mountainside grave.

TAR SPACKLED BANNER

Browsing my diary, I found the following blurb about "Freedom" under the date of entry for April Fool's Day 2026 A.D.:

D.E.: 4-01-2026—

Free's (damnbetcha!) become akin to my kin: a _kainga_ or "joking relative" as the Otong Javanese put it. We are "ink-brothers of the bad pun." Mingled our Mont Blanc pens' red ink, vowing to mangle language.

Today he brought over a pan of fresh-baked corn bread. He had "dis thang," as Don-de-bartender oft put it, for corn—ya peep? Always ate undercooked sausage hash with canned Mexicorn mixed in. He was corny, especially on April Fool's Day. Anyway, to make a long story short, I burnt my finnies on the pan. Later, I receiverooed a pingful punful e-mail message that read in red text:

He brot pain in a pan of bread.

I could just see him writing this, an undisguised play on the German, French, Spanish, and English words designating "bread": 3 right-hand finnies holding the mouse, 2 left-hand digits tapping the keys, his eyes see the words, his tongue pronouncing them as they are written, then lolling lazily across his surgically redone lips, while his body cramps from leaning over his too-small children's-size computer desk bought at an estate sale of a Jewish neighbor's stuff (the dude'd been blown to biteroos by dynamite wielding AmPats the week before).

TAR SPACKLED BANNER

As mucho on guarderoo I am for *pernipadnost* (Uterineroo criticism's term for "the pernicious patriarchal advent of nostalgia"), when I peep some of "Freedom's" youthful poems I just want to sing and sing *Auld Lang Syne*. Witness his tribute to Rabelais in *Paean to my Corn-Sausage Belly. Moreover.* It virtually anticipates the actual girth his stomach obtained later in life after removal of a monstrously long tape-worm from his intestine, unwittingly declaiming "Freedom's" *hamartia*, his tragic flaw, his passion for corn and undercooked sausage simultaneously accompanied by spoonfuls of strawberry shortcake:

> *The garden-sty of my belly lllllllllllllllllllllllllllllllllllllllllllllllllllifts.*
> *The garden-sty of my belly rrrrrrrrrrrrrrrrrrrrrrrrrrrrrrrrrises.*
> *The garden-sty of my belly rrrrrrrrrrrrrrrrrrrrrrrrrrrrrrrrreclines.*
> *The garden-sty of my belly is-a-bushhen's-nest-in-lifting.*
> *The garden-sty of my belly is-an-aaaaaaaaaaaaaaaaanthill.*
> *The garden-sty of my belly lifts-bbbbbbbbbbbbbbbbbends.*
> *The garden-sty of my belly is-an-ironwood-tree-in-lifting.*
> *The garden-sty of my belly lies-ddddddddddddddddddown.*
> *The garden-sty of my belly bbbbbbbbbbbbbbbbbburgeons.*

This bozotic aesthetic disphoria covers 2 of the 3 ol' aesthetic bases: art imitating art *and* life coming to imitate art. *Q.E.D.*

His fav author (not mine) was Bill H. Gass. Used to always, as Don put it, "pump dem Gass." We'd yell "Fill 'er up!" and he'd give us the Gass. After his bitter divorce from Clougdah "Hacker" Schorr, he'd oft tank up on a mixture of O.J. Bronco's and a dip from Gass's book *The Tunnel* (recited in stanzas):

> *I sleep alone now.*
> *With my clock.*
> *My clock has a tick wide as its ovaled face.*
> *I think you might call it a thock.*
> *But its thock is soft.*
> *Perhaps it thucks.*

So prodigious a plagiarist was he, so avidly did he cop from the *literati*, past and present, feet on bar-rail we'd declaim such truisms as:

> "You can't out run the cops!"

or

> "Arrested by the cops again!"

or

> "Cheese it, the cops!"

Assault and Battery (2029)
"Freedom" Trumpoulos throws leaking D-cell batteries into the Pacific Ocean, an illegal, long forbidden, Leaverite initiation ritual done as performance art

"Freedom's" father, Efthemios, had once been a member of Usonia's notorious Leavers. An anti-pan-capitalist/pro-pollution terrorist organization rooted in the 20th-century-economist Joseph Schumpeter's controversial notion that capitalism will be destroyed not by its failure, but by its very *success*. Contra the recombinant fascists, the Leavers had argued that sexual cleansing, racial cleansing, ethnic cleansing were heap fictional searcheroos for a purity that had never existerooed. *And never would.* Contra the Soft-Libs, they had argued that the welfare-state and reformism only aimed at softening the bad effecteroos of capitalism. Prolonging the time we suffered under its graby greederoo.

Leaverism—strongly opposed by Gaian Zenecology—proposed to accelerate the demise of capitalism by a *homeopathic solution to a pathetic home*. Their means? A passive-aggressive strategy for intensifying the pollution: "Leavering" your unsorted trash (full of nonbiodegradable items) and dangerous chemical wastes (carcinogenic preferred) in ponds, lakes, streams, and oceans. They had: fought recycling in all its formeroos, used flurocarbons, dumped leaking batteries in the oceans and inland waters, and done raindances to promote acid-rain. Detractors both on the Right and Left called them "Damn Homeos." "Freedom" loved 'em, loved to hear tales of their trashy exploits, even began a series of art performances in tribute to their long forbidden rituals. Ho! He was even arresterooed once. Ya peep?

If in the ecological sphere the Leavers had championed the increased destruction of our natural resources, in the political sphere they had urged voters to elect the heap blarghfulest of 80-column-minded candidates. They'd pointed to Chicagary politics as their *exemplum*. And, in the economic, they had praised extreme greederoo. Their Leaver Poster Series honored Ivana Trump and other Captains of Excess. They had felt that by stimulating the inherent vices of their sworn enemy—pan-capitalism—the quicker its resources would be exhausted; the faster it would be discredited, and collapse, heralding in a "hard-age" during which the inert masses would come alive and skipideedooda Usonia for eco-saferoo zones like Australia, New Zealand, and Tasmania.

How do you kill a glutton and get away with it? Feed him! How do you wipe out a bunker? Dig it deeper! is how the movement's leader, "Trash

Tory," had rationalized their methods. They had viewed themselves as true early-21st-century "anaecopatriots." Being in spasm—apathetic yet fully committed—they had spray-painted their mottoes—

LEAVER USONIA IF YA LOVE IT

and

DO TRASH 'N BE GOOD

—throughout Usonia.

When Leaver-taggers hit the White House in 2008 and left in their wake mucho graffiti and 5 heap biggeroo piles of asbestos, several Secret Service Agents lost their jobs. The Usonian F.B.I. and C.I.A. were told it was open season on Leavers. Thus beganeroo the Extraordinary Pacification Action (code name EPA) for the liquidation of the Leavers. Mass arrests. Shootings—supposedly only while escaping—and long prison terms the result. "Trash Tory" was taken prisoner at a landfill near the infamous Copper Basin in Ducktown, Tennessee. Tried by a kangaroo court of gumbies—the judge was a card-carrying member of Green Peace—he was given "short-life" in Illinois' old Joliet Prison. Stuffed in a cell filled to his waist with asbestos, discarded and pulverized laser-printer toner cartridges, and lead paint chips—he died 3 years later from raging lung and prostate cancer. A bozotic 16-year old high-school student who, during an interview on the nationally televised show "20/20 2000," had confessed that her stay at a Leaver summer camp (free to all children with last names of Leaver) had made her more aware—

> We think the world is made for us, and that everything we do is always right; we learned that we should try to liveroo a more Leaverish lifestyle. Ya peep?

—had also been arrested in the sweep. She and her father, Ishmael, were retroactively charged with sedition, and marcherooed past the Nova White House with the following placards dangling from their necks:

You Leaver It, You Leave It!

Finally deported to Greater Bosnia where they horribly "slo-died" (mercy killing denied them) after being caught in a Genemort attack 6 months later. The Leavers fared no better than had The Black Panthers of yore. Ya peep?

***Subjunctivity* (2030) "Freedom"
Trumpoulos, art performance
at Space Out Gallery, sponsored
by SACRE—BLEU and *Vogue***

"Freedom" perpetually utopia-touted what Rachel Blau DuPlessis had called "the time of the future perfect," the realm of a pingful subjunctivity (it *should and would be* better), as heap opposerooed to the dystopian future imperfect. He cranked *[thought]* that by making the present imperfect you assured (by some dialectical mumbo-jumbo) a pingful future. Hence, the rétro-Leaverist sympathies and the rétro-Futurist tenor of his several art performances sponsored and funded in part by the controversial art-support group called

SACRE—BLEU

(San Angelo Rétro-Contemporary Exhibitions —Backwards-Looking Ergo Utopian), largely funded itself by generous grants from the French Socialist L'Outrecuidant government. French President Jean-Jacques L'Outrecuidant, a former Rétro-French New Wave cinema star—despite heap blarghful EU *[European Union]* objections—embarassed Usonia's Art-megeddonism *[arts defunding]* by passing a sort of reverseroo Marshall Plan aimed at cultural support of non-fascist Usonian art whithering on the ultra-conservative pan-capitalist vine.

Ho! You say I do unpingfully digresseroo? Do you of the literary profes-soriat accuse me of "Maturin" too quickly, i.e., of cultivating dozens of shifting scenes, fantastic coils of tales-within-tales to sadly perplexeroo the Peeper as did the bozotic author of *Melmoth*, Charles Robert Maturin (1780 - 1824)? But if, as the elder-day adage doth say, a duderoo *is* what he eats, then he *is also* what his mates are. We do assimilate nutrients from both *food* and *friends*, ya peep?

What I assimilated from "Freedom" was appreciation of his chameleon charlatan self as the heapessential *[quintessential]* touting of a cobbled together and makeshift image of heap Postieish *[Postmodernist]* self-hood. His conscious, aesthetically constructed "borderline personality" revealed to me that our conventional notion of an *ego* is actually a species of hoodwinking, what the Tibetans term *dak dzin*, merely "grasping to a self" to constitute a delusory notion of "I" and "mine," self and other *[a notion that anticipated psychoanalyst Jacques Lacan's conception of the radically decentered subject]*. No surprise then that "Freedom" would subjunctively cajole me into playing dress up. At 1 point, he said I *would look* stunning wearing a powder-blue suit, with dark blue shirt, tie and handkerchief (for

The author as digi-piced by "Freedom" Trumpoulos holding the latter's prop while he works on his "Fountain of Youth," a series of digi-pics of handguns

***Fountain of Youth* (digi-pic-re-photo detail of an Andy Warhol litho, 2029) F. Trumpoulos**

wiping oil from those O.J. Bronco's off my lips), D-width black brogues, black wool socks with dark blue clocks on them (a reference to my interest in tempo-jumperooing). So I bought the garb. One day in late autumn when the year was dying early, the leaves were falling fast (for California), outside his gloomy Glendale studio in clear bright sunlight, "Freedom" digi-piced me in an awkward pose wearing the aforementioned outfit. This, while he was finishing up on his "Revenge of the Action Painters" series (see front cover image where a Jasper Johns painting of the U.S. flag has been Jackson Pollockized) and starting to workeroo on a series of gun images (barrel always pointing upward) titled "Fountain of Youth" for, according to him: "The handgun provides youth a means of staying forever young—as corpses!"

So! Ho! What's the sum? Why I've learnerooed from reading the bozotic suffering Surealist poet Antonin Artaud that:

All writing is pig shit.

Confirmed it, damnbetcha, by writing Uterineroo theory/criticism. And from "Freedom's" example, heap discoverooed that:

The ego is heap biggest pig of all.

Confirmed it by writing this autobio.

Aye! For the postmodernishly over-educated, the mysterious textual aporia *[contradictions]* of this, my endeavoroo, is the very bozotic facteroo that *despite* assimilating "Freedom's" anti-egoic exemplum, this me-ego is writing this, my autobio. Ya peep?

*　　　*　　　*

TAR SPACKLED BANNER

II

Honest labor and the sweat of your brow will in many cases earn you a progressively lower standard of living and an uncertain future for whatever children you are optimistic enough to bring into a democracy in which most people are created unequal.
        —Carol Squiers, "At Their Mercy: A Reading of Pictures
              From 1988"

There goes one ready equally for doing or suffering, and of whom we shall soon hear that he is involved in some great catastrophe—it may be of deep calamity—it may be of memorable guilt.
        —Sister Apollonia, Mother Superior of St. Blaise's High
              School upon witnessing Mark Durfuherman's graduation

Ho! I crank it was said by a relative of Mark Durfuherman that "He was the idiot of the family." But, according to my father, so was I—keeping in minderoo that this "I" ("that little changeling, the 'subject'," as Nietzsche put it) is a ho-hum Humean Human fiction caused by grrrrammar, an aggressive epiphenomenon of language. In facteroo, we both had internalized the maternal rub-a-dubby, clang-a-lang rhythms of heap bozotic thyroid blondes, thin and nervous mamas who rode blarghfully bumpy public transportation while pregnant—his ma in Perth Amboy, New Jersey, mine in Chicagary, Illinois—while systematically denying us after breaching the meager breasteroo in favor of the brown rubber and milky plastic simulacrum. As Jean-Paul "Skew-eye" Sartre so eloquently stated it in his late text, *The Idiot of the Family*:

Jean-Paul Sartre (UPI)

His own mother, engulfed in the depths of his body, becomes the pathetic structure of his affectivity. . . . The prehistoric past comes back to the child like Destiny.

And ho! What a destiny for me, for Durfuherman! Ya peep? Probably why we both demanded the vibrations of little model train sets when we reacherooed the age of reason and had the itch to travel. While

My model train set, San Angelo (2017)

Mark Durfuherman next to his *Nordlandz* train complexus somewhere in Montana (2007)

gave my train set up at puberty, he *never* did, perpetually expanding it. By 2007, he'd built a huge train complexus he'd dubbed *Nordlandz*. The monthly mag, *Model Railroader* (May, 2008) described this heap huge utopian train simenvironment thus:

> What with its 8 miles of flextrack, 500,000 trees, 135 continuously running trains, 4,000 buildings, 350 bridges, Nordlandz, built of balsa wood, heap defies description. One the 1 hand it's an HO model railroad, but it's like no layout you've ever peeped or probably even imaginerooed. This is more like something you'd have expected to peep at Usonia's Disney World prior to its take-over by the Christian Right and its change to God's World. On the other hand, it's envisioned as a train-utopia likes of which haven't been imagined since Albert Speer peererooed down on his li'l architectural model of the New Berlin. In its center, near towering double cantilever span recalling Scotland's Firth of Forth Bridge—seen by White Supremacists as a symbol of White ingenuity—resides Durfuherman's proposed fasci-headquarters, a baronial chateau on a mountainous island keep fed by train bridges from 5 directions. In sum, Durfuherman envisions his Fasci-Free State as a vast complex of train tracks spanning the former states of Wyoming, Idaho, and Montana with its skyscraper intensive capital, Gorgeous, located at the head of a deep gorge criss-crossed with track 'n trestle.

Facteroo: I've always suspected something heap blarghful at work in the psyche of adults who still build train sets, don engineer's cap, hoot 'n toot with the trains, and have a life-time subscription to *Model Railroader*. The fasci-case of Mark Durfuherman does heap confirmeroo my suspeeps *[suspicions]*.

Nordlandz, the skyscraper capital city of Gorgeous and track-spanned
gorge laid out far below shows Mark Durfuherman's train-mania

TAR SPACKLED BANNER

To build his fantastic dreams, Durfuherman proposed to hired cheap Turkish labor—the 21st-century version of Chinese "coolies" who, he felt, would jumperoo at the chance to escape the blarghful horrors of the Turko-Bosnian front. Once the project was completed and hundreds of Turkish emigrés were behind his electrified fences, he would make his infamous Modest Proposal, asking of them: "*Avrupalilaştirilamiyanlardanmisiniz?*" (Turkish for "Are you one of those who can't be Europeanized?"), then offering them their choice of being either strangled on the spot or becoming Born-Again Christians; even the easier alternative had its condition—namely, that they must be bounderoo before a magistrate to convert 20 Muslims a day, on their return to Turkey. These 20, it was reasoned, will convert 20 mucho more apiece, and these 200 converts, converting their due number in the same time, all Turkey would be converted before the Grand Signior knew where he was! Then would comeroo the *coup d'éclat*—1 fine morn every minaret in Istanbul was to ring out with bells, instead of the cryeroo of the Muezzins.

Durfuherman's *Nordlandz* showing his baronial chateau on an island keep called "Humpy-Dump Island," fed by 5 railroad bridges (Rebel Year 1)

TAR SPACKLED BANNER

Who exactly was this doofus Durfuherman? I once sat down at my modular rétro Dymaxion office-nook. Fashioned, natch, by underpaid Brazilian Indians out of the finest, rarest rainforest hardwoods. Booted up my Taco Bell computer, brushing off an Asian gyspy moth *[have they become pervasive?]*. Before the desktop's icons appeared, the daily 'A Question of Inspiration' (red text on green field) queried:

<LICKED CORRECT BOOTS & STEPPED ON IMPIOUS FACES TODAY?>

I keyed in my secret password—**D-U-M-B-O-X**—logging onto the Globo-Com Net. Index finger touched the Netucantescape 50.2 browser icon on the desktop, an animated nostalgia disaster picture (2015 A.D.) of a comet ramming the ill-fated MIR III space station. Home page depicting grunge rockeros on the edge of a cliff appeared. Ran a URA-Yahoo net-search for info on that notorious 21st-century blackguard Mark Durfuherman. A long list of items and a mugshot came up on-screen. I clicked on *CURRICULUM VITAE.* Up popped the following. Load time only 7 minutes (usually 15)!

CURRICULUM VITAE

Mark Durfuherman
A.K.A. "Der Bulle"
alias, "Mufti Penner"
b. Perth Amboy., N.J. 1970 – d. San Quentin, 2011
Male, 5' 9", 180 lbs., dark hair and blue eyes
Incarcerated: Folsom Prison for 3 years for aggravated assault and attempted murder while serving as a police officer in San Angelo, he authored *The Ex-Inmate's Complete Guide to Successful Employment and Deployment* (1998).
Synopsis:

Strong confidence level; good communicator;

Not afraid to speak up or ask questions;

Self-motivated; not easily intimidated;

Follows directions; clever & creative;

Works extremely well independently;

Thrives on commission sales; handles stress;

Good sense of time management;

Excellent physical condition;

Mechanically inclined; can make hard

decisions; resourceful; can be counted

on to get the job finished.

TAR SPACKLED BANNER

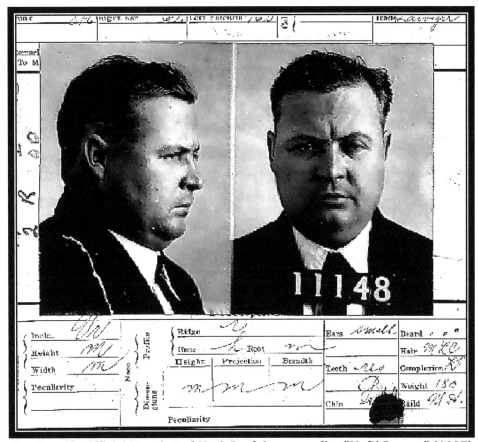

San Quentin Official Mugshot of Mark Durfuherman, alias "Mufti Penner" (1997)

For Durfuherman—that advocate of "Dust and Rust, Grease and Crime"—a real rail rhizome was to replaceroo the Internet in Durfurman's Fasci-Free State. Intertrackuality was to replace intertextuality. It was rumored by hackers that he had a super sub-minus 80-column, HO gauge mind and so

was incapable of memorizing the mucho characters in the net URLs, nay, even incapable of *typing* them in without agitation and making heaps of mistakeroos. They said it was due to his childhood habit of Testors' glue and paint sniffing; he claimed this was becauseroo his small daughter was named Dot and he had a Puritanical, anti-incestual aversion to saying or typing the proverbial *dot com* in URLs. Maybe why he reacted heap blarghfully to pro-Internet, *Wired* peeper Corman the Scald's ill-fated visit to his stronghold. Nothing more deliciously blow-a-fuse vicious, get-up-steam sadismeroo, than a moronhood violated by being challenged to crank *[think]* heap mucho than it's circuitry is electrically capable of handling. Ya peep?

The author's tie-dye T-shirt

Fasci-Free State Border Patrol cruiser with Durfuherman's blarghful "White Pride" logo

Ho, dear Peeper! You accuseroo this concatenation of pingful and blarghful habits, odors, and perceptions of yet digressing, perpetually deferring my own auto-yak *[autobiography]*? You must peep that the self is peeped only through *the other*. And who could be mucho more *other* to me that *Herr* Durfuherman? I still wear a tie-dye T-shirt whose pingful pattern is the Hippy's proverbial rétro-perfect peace symbol. Durfuherman placed his "White Pride" Celtic cross on all his T-shirts, even on the Fasci-Free State's border patrol cars, etc. I avidly read the Spanish philosopher of strife—Miguel De Unamuno—I recrank *[re-call]* a nip apropos this very text-eroo:

Can I be as I believe myself or an others believe me to be? Here is where these line become a confession in the presence of my unknown and unknowable me, unkown and unknowable for myself. Here is where I create the legend wherein I must bury myself.

Durfuherman, the fascist revolutionary, was often digi-piced holding a well-thumberooed copy of a *Cliff Notes* (2000) synposis of *[Carl Von]* Clausewitz's 1832 classic *On War*; an excerpt that might have interesterooed him:

Revolutionary wars are not 'Clausewitzian' wars of sovereign states fighting each other for the usual objectives. Strategies and tactics used by 1 side are not those used by the other. Technical superiority invariably belongs to the side which seeks to suppress a revolution. But, the 'military forces' of the revolutionary adversary are diffuse. One is never sure whether one has destroyed them unless one is ready to destroy a large portion of the population, and this usually conflicts with the political aim of the war and hence also violates a fundamental Clausewitzian principle.

TAR SPACKLED BANNER

I teacheroo advanced plagiarism and, unabashedly, steal freely from a myriad of sources for my own unoriginally original writerly writings. But rebelling Durfuherman—taking advantage of the chaos following the 2008 eruption of Mt. St. Helens—boldly ripped off 3 states, ransoming recalcitrant politicos, businessmen, and Usonian government-gumbies for mucho sums to financeroo his Confederate air force and Neo-Panzer armor. Satellite surveillance some months after Durfuherman's Rebellion successfully led Idaho, Montana, and Wyoming out of the Union showed the hippity-quick blarghful military build-up of the rebel forces and impelled Usonian forces to

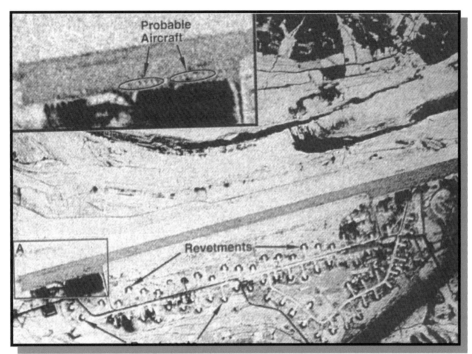

A Usonia C.I.A. satellite digi-pic of an airfield near Durfuherman's Free-State headquarters near what was formerly Bozeman, Montana (2009)

attackeroo. *Moreover.* It later came out that the attack was really motivated spy reports that Durfuherman had been reading a *Cliff Notes* summary of Herman Kahn's *On Thermonuclear War* and possibly planned to manufacture a Doomsday Device out of nuclear weapons commandeered from the military installations in his sphere of influence. Attack the rebellious Fasci-Free State or try to dismantle the device and—so it goes—

KABLOOY ! EVERYONE GETS TO CALL IN SICK.

Global nuclear war clouds—*Ach! Eine wunderschöne Aussicht* [a beautiful view]*!* Or so cranked *Herr* Durfuherman.

TAR SPACKLED BANNER

The wars waged by the United States in the 19th century were punitive or exterminating actions against Native inhabitants, an unsuccessful expedition against Canada in 1812 (but we did get our *revanche* mucho later in terms of acid rain), and easy wars of conquest against Mexico and the moribund Spanish empire. From there on we peeped war—the Civil War, WWI, WWII, Korea, and Viet Nam—as justified less for the national interest than for heap-peeps *[important ideological reasons]*. But Grenada, Panama, the Gulf War, and the Bosnian Conflict were (*is* in the case of the latter) fought more for Clauswitzian "reasons of state." So it was refreshing for a changeroo to think once again about having a real bimbop bangeroo brawl over heap-peeps. *In that corner we have Mark Durfuherman and The Fasci-Free State. In this corner we have Usonia and its favorite son* [sic] *. . .*

Well, who *did* take up the gauntlet for Usonia and strikeroo the first blow? Not the Feds whose gumby leadership was of questionable loyalty; not the National Guard whose rank and file were pure docile social body, mucho too sympathetic to The Rebellion's basic principles to plugeroo fellow M&M's *[manical monoculturalists]* on the up-and-up—ya peep? No, the taskeroo fell to someone "with the X-nature." A loner hailing originally from Stickney, Illinois. A scholar of ebonics. A nautical autodidact who sailed solo to New Zealand so as to study eco-foresty. Ho! No other than **Charles Cane Forester** who, recallerooing the Lincoln Brigade of Spanish Civil War fame, recruited a rag-tag gaggle of:

> writerly Writers
> unemployed Liberals
> pejorative Performance Artists
> nubilous Patriots
> militant Quakers
> lethal Lesbians
> jocose Johnnies
> impecunious Actors
> harassed School Teachers
> greedy Mercenaries
> gallant Gays
> fringe Elements
> esteemed Professors
> dangerous Street People
> committed Commies
> bozotic Border Brujos
> and all-vegan Green Peacer Eco-Terrorists

that he whipped into that lean mean wonky anti-fascist fighting machine:
The North Usonia Loyalist Alliance Freedom Brigage.
Its acronym being **NULLAFREBIE**, Loyalist troopers were often—too bad Galahad—unjustly dubbed "Nulls" by the unsympathetic or the unimpressed.

TAR SPACKLED BANNER

Another down-loaderoo from Globo-Com Net:

 WELCOME TO *ENCYCLOPEDIA UNSONIA* BRIEFS ON-LINE

"We have remodeled the Alhambra with our steam-shovels and we are proud of our yardage."
—President Berzilius "Coach" Windrip

FILE RETRIEVED: **FORESTER, CHARLES, CANE**

NICKNAME "CHUCK"

B. STICKNEY, IL, MARCH 21,1970 - D. D.C., ARBORETUM, MARCH 15, 2013
B.S. DEGREE IN EBONICS, UNIVERSITY OF ILLINOIS, CHICAGO
M.S. DEGREE IN ECO-FORESTRY, UNIVERSITY OF AUCKLAND, NEW ZEALAND
(THESIS: "GLOBAL WARMING: ON THE POSSIBILITIES OF ANTARCTIC FORESTS")
CONTINUE? Y/N
Y

"Better injustice than disorder."
—President Berzilius "Coach" Windrip

LITTLE IS KNOWN OF FORESTER'S EARLY LIFE. AFTER HE FINISHES GRADUATE SCHOOL, HE PILGRIMAGES TO AYERS ROCK TO STUDY THE MYSTERIOUS ALPHABET OM THAT HUGE BOULDER IN THE CENTRAL DESERT OF AUSTRALIA. HIS ODD BEHAVIOR WINS HIM THE TITLE OF "THE SPARTAN SYBARITE,"

RETURNING TO USONIA, HE RAPIDLY BECOMES A LEADING ANTI-FASCIST AGITATOR AND SPOKESPERSON DURING "THE TROUBLES."

DURING HIS MILITARY CAMPAIGNS, HE MASTERS "TETRACEREBROFASCITOMY" (THE ART OF SPLITTING A FASCIST'S HEAD FOUR WAYS WITH A LOGGER'S AX) AND IS GENERALLY FEARED.

TAR SPACKLED BANNER

> HE WAS DESCRIBED BY FRIENDS AS: "A LION IN WAR, A SWEET LAMB IN PEACE; HARSH IN BATTLE, YET DEVOUT IN PRAYER; FEROCIOUS TO HIS ENEMIES, BUT FULL OF KINDNESS TOWARD HIS BROTHERS AND ALL TREES."
>
> IN 2011, HE AND HIS COHORTS ARE GIVEN A LAND-GRANT AND THEY FOUND THE ECOSOCIAL UTOPIA CALLED 'ARBORETUM" BASED ON FORESTER'S ECOSOCIOPOLITICAL TRACT "DA FOUNDIN' PRINCIPLES O' DA BRANCHLAND." HIS DICTUM: "GOOD METHODS BE BRINGIN' GOOD STRUCTURES" IS OFT CITED EVEN TODAY IN HIS HOMELAND.
>
> IT IS IS RUMORED FORESTER WAS A CLANDESTINE MEMBER OF THE NEO-KNIGHTS TEMPLARS, ALHOUGH HIS OFFICIAL RELIGIOUS AFFLIATION WAS THE ECO-BAHA'I FAITH.
>
> ON THE ANNIVERSARY OF FORESTER'S DEATH, ARBORETIANS RECITE THE FOLLOWING PLATITUDE: "GOD BE MAKIN' DA COUNTRY, HERMANS *[MAN]KIND* BE MAKIN' DA TOWN, BUT FORESTER BE MAKIN' BOTH, 'N WE BE CALLIN' IT 'DA BRANCHLANDO'."
>
> (TO PEEP MORE DATA ON THIS ENTRY, PURCHASE OUR CD-ROM ENCYCLOPEDIA)
>
> ———————————————————
>
> PUBLIC SERVICE MESSAGE OF THE DAY:
>
> "IT IS UNNECESSARY TO EVOKE SPIRITUAL POWERS
>
> WHEN MACHINES GIVE MUCHO BETTER RESULTS."

What had brought such opposing figures into vicious conflict? An outline of why the Durfuherman's of Usonia were in such a dither should list:

I. Affect-determined repugnance of pan-capitalism:
   a) low economic expectations
   b) whithering up of the labor unions
   c) global economy replacing a national economy
   d) service-oriented jobs, often temporary or part-time
   e) these meager jobs threatened by ethnic and racial minorities

II. Assuming a Neo-Clausewitzian *legitimacy* of hawkish attitudes:
   a) antipathy of the attempts to outlaw war and to establish a
      machinery of international law (e.g., the United Nations)
   b) the identification of anti-Communism with the defense of
      Western Civilization and the White Race
   c) the insistence that the magnitude and the intensity of war
      can be controlled

III. The spread of Christian Identity Bible-Belt consciousness:
   a) the weakening of the Enlightenment meta-narratives
      of emancipation and progress via rational means
   b) without legitimate rational foundations, dogma comes
      to replace "liberal humanism"

    c) faith in the lay interpretation of The Bible replaces the scholarly rigor and the scientific method of Modernity

    d) Federalism is replaced by a preferred allegiance to The Kingdom of Heaven

    e) anti-Semitism (the Jews as "Satan's Spawn" syndrome)

    f) anti-gay and lesbian paranoia

IV. *Posse Comitatus* "Almost Heaven" consciousness:

    a) hostility toward the Federal government (The Civil War of yore continues) and its minions on a myriad of issues:

        i) taxation

        ii) representation

        iii) segregation

        iv) school prayer

        v) abortion

        vi) cultural funding

        vii) right to bear arms

        viii) FBI and CIA powers

        ix) AIDS as government plot to reduce population, etc.

    b) radical democracy (for Starchy Whites only) arising from the County level, the traditional level of Klan terrorism

    c) increased S.P.I.K.E. (Specially Prepared Individuals for Key Events) paramilitary training for all ages

    d) canonization of *Posse Comitatus* legends: martyr Gordon Kahl and ex-Special Forces founder of elder-day's "Almost Heaven" paramilitary complex, Col. James "Bo" Gritz

 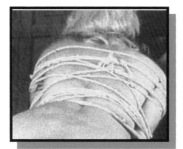

Disaffected Gen-XX Youth   **Female Fasci-Free State Hostage in bondage**

V. Mini-Free State Worship and the Assertion of the Self Contra The Bunker State:

    a) cellular development of resistance against an incumbent political regime expanding to overt resistance by small armed bands and insurrection to create the fasci-mini-state

    b) state worship allows the *assertion* of the self; albeit

dissolved into the mini-secessionist free state, but still differentiated from *other selves* (the enemy) and magnified in power by numbers of believers

c) mini-state worship offers an outlet for boundless love and boundless hate, both passions elevated to sacred duties

d) clannishness becoming Klannishness

d) rejection of academic jargon and subtle cranking as found in Bernard Crick's touting of Humanist politics in his *Defense of Politics* (1962; reprint 2004):

Politics is a bold prudence, a diverse unity, an armed conciliation, a natural artifice, or creative compromise and a serious game on which free civilization depends; it is a reforming conserver, a sceptical believer and a pluralistic moralist; it has a lively sobriety, a complex simplicity, an untidy elegance, a rough civility and an everlasting immediacy . . .

Recombinant fascism's succinct translation would be:

Shoot 'em all and let God sort 'em out later.

e) identification through a jargon and an argot; sympathy through song and poems; note the following fasci-poem attributed to Cormac the Scald:

TAR SPACKLED BANNER

Through Night and Blood to Light
(Durch Nacht und Blut zur Licht)

Ho! The full heart of the Freeman—
Through the black night red with blood—
Pure White does pour out of a Rednecky tongue.
In faggy quips is froggy French well-spoken,
And musical is the Wop's garlic'd speech.
But when the glance is turned pingfully heavenward,
As when the Klan do swear their allegiance,
The Rednecky word sounds like the metal of their swords
With which they will smote the blarghful stranger's yoke.
So then hear them Wigger's weep—ya peep?

f) politics as a zero-sum game—whatever benefits 1 side,
   hurts the other—encourages:
      i) *Us* versus *Them* paranoid siege-mentality
      ii) Krugerand investment versus the stock market
      iii) "Chicken" jousting head-on in cars for sport

TAR SPACKLED BANNER

III

O da terrible influence o' this race which do be servin' neither Gaia nor disputin' Maya, be given o'er to da mundane sciences, to base mechanical professions! Pernicious breed, indeed! What will you be not attemptin', left to your own devices, abandon'd without restraint to that fatal spirit o' badknowledge, o' invention, o' progress.
— Charles Forester, *Scathin' Letters to Uitlanders* (2012)

What makes fascism dangerous is its molecular or micropolitical power, for it is a mass movement: a cancerous body rather than a totalitarian organism. American film has often depicted these molecular focal points: band, gang, sect, family, town, neighborhood, vehicle fascisms spare no one.
— G. Deleuze and F. Guattari, *A Thousand Plateaus* (1980)

And so it goes. Separatist paranoia poisons Usonia, while ozone poisons the yellow pines. Blarghful paramilitary escalation. Blarghful pollution on the increase. Texas heap seceded from the Union. Bing-bang-boom, Idaho-Montana-Wyoming followed suit. I reacherooed the age of reason and studied my Neo-Catholicism Catechism, but refuserooed the Communion wafer when the religious chips were down. Ho! I was matcherooed in a vehement religious war contra my parents, while Charles Cane Forester was matcherooed in a deadly anti-fascist agon against his blarghful ideological oppositeroo, Mark "Monty" Durfuherman.

The Aging Charles C. Forester

In 2009, on the anniversary of the Kent State National Guard killings of protesting students, Forester delivered an addresseroo to a group of disaffected, stick 'n stone-throwing, Gen-XXers on that very campus in the (bleak) hope of garnering more volunteers for his NULLAFREBIE forces, this after their blarghful winter campaign in Idaho which Usonian military historians have since dubbed "Retreat from Yellow Pine":

TAR SPACKLED BANNER

Sticks & Stones Do Be Breakin' Da Bones,
But Da Branches Do Be Ne'er Hurtin' Me.

Terrorism, as da function o' periphery versus da center, whether do be state-sponsor'd or its contrary, now do seem to be da subset o' those twin affections o' da 20th century, as least as Martin Heidegger do put it: boredom 'n terror. As such, they do seem to be intimately be tie, as either da promotion o' or da reaction formation to, da telematic presence which do now circle da globe—thanks to Globo-Com—da grip o' which do daily tighten. Terror do be now almost fully da spectacular statistical entity, almost da sublime in its large-numbers ability to numb da brain with da with da fog-like insistence, obscurin' 'n highlightin' da features at da same time in what do be perfect example o' da 'spasmic' mode of consciousness so prevalent today.

But our notion o' da perfect socius do be to make life do be heap less panic-stricken, violent, 'n base, yet not be less energetic; to be shiftin' da incidence o' struggle fer existence from our lower to our higher emotions, so we do anticipate 'n do neutralize da motives o' da cowardly 'n da bestial, that da ambitious 'n energetic imagination which do be hiswoman's finest quality do may become da incentive 'n da determinin' factor in survival. We be need true science o' becomin' in order to assemble our pleasure without garnishin' it with da moral tutelage. Ya grok? ...

The Response

Cries of "pure octal-forty"

Cries of "Ho! Go back Down-Under"

Glork! Committing error-33, Forester had predicted recruitment success at Kent upon his earlier success at Tuskeegee. As detailed in that scholarly redaction of Forester's writings, *Da Green Book,* due to his bozotically ebonic diction and his firm optimistic rejection of Sturgeon's Law ("90% of every-thing is crap"), local Skinheads attending the former—clad in Fred Perry shirts, Doc Marten boots, Levi jeans and waving White Pride flags—were hostile. Starchy Whites cries of "Do da ol' 'bout-face 'n go back Down-Under,

TAR SPACKLED BANNER

Buried Shed (1970) Robert Smithson

you blarghy Wigger, or we'll bury you like *that* blarghy shed over there" filled the terrorist-resistent auditorium (located near the site of conceptual artist Robert Smithson's controversial 1970 earthwork *Buried Shed*). Ho! Even the culti-multuralist sympatheticos tossed up their hands, kicked up their feet and got quizzical expressions on their faces; ho! they admitted their 80-column minds were drawing a ho-heap blankeroo: "Hands off the gas, Bubby. You're pumpin' pure octal forty, ya peep?"

Black T-shirt clad student security had to keep the 2 jostling and disparate groups apart (see the previous paired images) and away from a stunnerooed Charles Forester who later described the air inside as "still, heavy 'n, despite da August humidity outside, parch'd with what do be feelin' like da breath o' da Australasian sirocco." Forester bravely, it was reported, hitched up his faded forest-green bell-bottoms and continued his yak-yak:

> *Durin' these days o' Da Troubles, our anti-fascist North Usonia Loyalist Alliance Freedom Brigade do be da thin line o' sufferin' 'n ill-arm'd humans be standin' 'tween fasci-barbarism 'n eco-decency.You do be can be part o' his dream. Join NULLA-FREBIE 'n peep da Big Trees, sting da fasci-creeps like Bumbly Bees.*
>
> *Now our branchly lifeworld do be only chang'd limb by limb, not as da whole trunk. We do be like da ship on its way out o' San Francisco Bay: we be not able to tear da ship down 'n rebuild it on da open sea, but we do be can repair or change it part by part while we do be travelin', workin' on 1 part while relyin' on da other parts to be sustainin' us. Possibilities do be unlimit'd 'cept by da scarcity o' da ideas 'n da materials. Ya peep?*
> *. . .*

He wound his yak down with an appeal to Ecozen consciousness:

> *If we do be have intuitive 'n imaginative feelin' o' da whole world as enfold'd in us, we will sense ourselves to be 1 with this world 'n feel heap genuine love fer it. Cease da day 'n bring on da night, if we don't be enfold'd in our world, in other people, 'n in nature as da whole! We do believe in Da Gaia thesis, da biosphere do form da single entity or natural system. . . .*

Forester concluded the tumultuous evening with an Ecozen koan attributed to the attentive heart of Ecozen monk, Stephanie Kaza:

TAR SPACKLED BANNER

If I do be findin' peace in da clearin', then what do be my relationship with wood—ya peep?

"This mystical tidbit," the student paper said, "kept the exiting audience scratcherooing their noggins as if they had heaps of blarghful head-lice."

Throughout the near debacle Forester kept his perception and judgement steady. Like the needle of the compass in a storm-tossed ship. So despite, or maybe because of the explosive situation, Forester's effect upon the crowd was like the movement of a great body, slower, but more irresistible.

Pingful suprise—the following day 23 volunteers signed up for NULLAFREBIE basic training in the Portland district staging area of North Usonia. After swearing allegiance to the anti-fascist cause in front of Smithson's funerealish earthwork, they were heap rouseroo-welcomed into the red pantalooned ranks by the presiding Colonel, F.N. Maude Jr.:

Therefore ariseroo, thou Sons of Usonia!
Brace thine arm for boom-bangeroos;
Nerve thy heart to meet, as things alike to thee,
Pingful pleasure or blarghy pain,
Profit or ruin, victory or defeat.
So minded, gird thee to the fight,
For so thou shalt not sineroo. Ya peep?

NULLAFREBIE insignia

In interviews on Globo-Com's "20/20 2000" the raw recruits, prior to hopping Jump-jet transports for the West Coast, cited the *vivifying* principles of war—"greed of honor and hankering after glory"—as reason for their enlistment. Ho! Whether these youth had the presence of mind, the *coup d'oeil,* the energy, firmness, staunchness, and character to overcome the danger, physical effort, uncertainty, and chance involved in armed conflict would be later tested—and proven—in such blarghy blood-baths as "Wipe out at Warren Ridge." Here's a description of that battle as taken from my uncle Neander Storch's journal. His given name had been Anders, but when he got tangled up in Forester's forest-fresh utopo-vision, he copped the name "Neander" ("New Man") from Dryden's "Essay of Dramatic Poesy." A part-time professor of English Lit at Occidental College in the San Angelo Metroland Basin, he'd volunteerooed early on in the conflict. He was a Captain at the tempo he made this entry:

TAR SPACKLED BANNER

Warren Campaign Begins

Uncle Neander's Artillery unit opens fire against The Skin Division at Warren Ridge

4/1/09—Day 3, The Warren Campaign

Ho! My most trusted platoon leader, 1st Lt. Nouphone Senemuongdong, was killed today by a sniper's bullet. As a small child he'd escaped the Killing Fields of his homeland—only to die here.

Ho! As I approached the bloody ridge I heard the thunder of both our artillery and theirs becoming plainer and plainer, followed by the howling and zip-zip of shrapnel which began to fall around me. I hastened to the hill where stood our great Chief, C.C. Forester. There the close striking of the large shells and the burting mortar shells was so frequent that the seriousness of life makes itself felt upon even the most hardened NULLAFREBIE trooper. Suddenly a mate known to me fell, a shell striking amongst the grouped troopers, causing some involuntary movements: everything from diving for cover, to spasms of pain, to the horizontal jig danced by torsi with missing limbs. I began to feel that I am no longer perfectly at ease and collected; even the bravest of us are somewhat confused, so I don't feel ashamed I soiled my pantaloons.

I took a step farther into the battle, which is still raging before us like a scene in a theater or a passage from Herr Von Clausewitz's book "On War." Division Commander, Col. James Omar "Pinky" Pinson, a man of acknowledged bravery, always kept carefully behind rising ground, a house, a tree, changed his "Depends" undergarments twice—a sure sign of increasing danger. Shrapnel rattled on the roofs of long-abandoned mountain cabins and their outmoded outhouses and fell in the fields; shells howled over us and ploughed the air in all directions. Ho! Soon there was the frequent sound of whistling bullets.

TAR SPACKLED BANNER

Ho! I stepped further towards the troops' front lines—closer than artillery officers like to go—to that sturdy infantry which for hours has maintained its firmness under this heavy fire; there the air was filled with the hissing of projectiles of all manner which announced their deadly proximity by a short sharp noise as they passed within an inch of my ear, nip at my dripping nose and heaving breast.

Ho! Pity at the sight of the maimed and fallen. One realizes the light of reason doesn't move here in the same medium, it is not refracted in the same manner as in speculative contemplation. . . .

Warren Ridge was a pingful, decisive victory for the NULLS that made defeat of Durfuherman's Rebellion only a matteroo of dinky tick-tocks *[a short time]*. Dispiriting reports ascended like smoke from the battered Freemen's front lines until, in 2010, Dur-fuherman's Rebellion was defeaterooed.

Durfuherman Caged (2010)

The day Durfuherman was found by my lucky uncle's division—hiding in a pigsty, smeared with pigshit, playing a banjulele — and arrested for treason, I turned 5 years old and ate heaps of insta-poppy seed cake and synth-vanilla ice cream out of 1 of my ma's antiques, an orange Fiesta Ware bowl. I liked the distinctive sound my little metal spoon made against its sides.

For his initiative, valor, and mercy shown to the civilian populace in the Warren Campaign—he had lumps of bread and cheese, kegs of beer and milk distributed after seeing a gaunt woman signify "a bleeding famine decked in sackcloth" by sticking a small French bun on the top of a fishing rod which she'd streaked with red spray paint and attached a shred of black electricians tape—Uncle Neander was promoted to major. To cheers, he was mustered out of the NULLAFREBIES 4 months later. Stories about his kindness as well as his bravery were circulated for years among friend and foe. Prematurely gray due to his battle experiences, he was peeped by his friends as "the good, gray Major." In 2012, he jumped ocean to England and retired handsomely—due to the criminally favorable exchange rateroo between dollars and pounds—on his military pensioneroo at 2 Tippintock's Gardens, Ligg's Walk, Clapham Rise. In an academically obscure letter from these nova digs to my baffled mother, he confessed:

> *I love to be in such places where there is no rat-a-tating of machine guns, nor rumbling of artillery, or crunching of tank wheels; mepeeps, here I may, without much molestation write my monograph on H. L. Hunt's visionary Alpaca [a self-published Randian utopian novel by Hunt, the second wealthest man in the world when the book was originally published in 1960, which gives its citizenry more votes per person the more money that person earns]. Here I can be cranking [thinking] what I am, whence I came, what I have done . . . here I may crank, and break at heart, and melt in my spirit, until my peepers become like 'the fishpools of Heshbon'. Ya peep?*

Before my uncle and his troops were disbanded, they witnessed Forester's optimistic words—his *last* to his battle-weary troops as NULLAFREBIE Supreme Commander, his *first* to his optimistic contingent of utopian Zenecology followers:

> *Da city do be must be made containable*
> *Regression to eco-safety do be heap insatiable*
> *'N so we do be climbin' up da utopia takable*
> *Like da ol' branch, unbreakable—to Da Branchland.*
> *Our nova home—ya peep?*

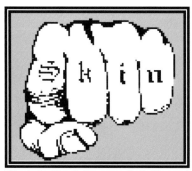

Sketch, Durfuherman's tattooed left fist as it appeared in *People* e-zine on December 20, 2010

After the fall of the Fasci-Free State, I bubble *[remember]* as a heap Komputer-kind—ho!—hypertexterooing through *People* e-zine for pix of beloved Uncle Neander. Ho! A whole issue in which the greedy editors had played to their peeperoos' voyeur-erooism by running a miscellany of click-able, downloadable images concerning the life and arrest of "Monty" Durfuherman, sketches of his bozotic tattooes, pix of his *Nordlandz* trainset, and the dead and debris from his ill-fated break-away Fasci-Free State.

TAR SPACKLED BANNER

**THE WRECKED
REBELLION**
(*People* e-zine)

**Fasci-Free State Party
Headquarters was
demolished**

**Durfuherman's
'Skins' Division
is taken
prisoner
by
NULLAFREBIE
troops**

In 2011, a year after clandestine negotiations with the Usonian Federal government, the following newspaper article appeared world-wideroo:

NEW USONIAN MOVEMENT

(AP NEWS)   NORTH USONIA. Large numbers of men and women from all parts of the world, including immigrants from Scotland's Findhorn Community, are uniting for the purpose of making a practical attempt to solve the eco-social problems of our day. The renewal of the liberal spirit of eco-social experiment once again sparks the imaginations of the members of 'Green Peace' and 'Green Thumb' who only recently have laid down their arms to re-establish harmony now that Idaho and Montana's fascist 'Free Amerika Movement' has been put down by the liberal 'Eco-Forces,' and Texas's invasion of Mexico has been repelled, albeit Texas's secession yet remains to be resolved. Such liberal forces, you recall, were largely drawn from Loyal North Usonians (formerly Northern California, Oregon, and Washington), who all fought bravely under the auspices of the North Usonia Loyalist Alliance Freedom Brigade.

The official date of the inauguration of this 'utopia,' as some term it, is set for the same date as the long-awaited execution of the notorious fascist rebel leader and ex-Los Angeles police officer, Mark Durfuherman. Durfuherman, you recall, was responsible for the devastating fire that swept South Chicagary 3 years ago, killing 300 people which signaled Texas's secession and the start of a myriad of brush-fire fascist rebellions across Usonia.

Arboretum's brave Ecotopist leader, Charles Forester, attacked Usonia: 'It do once be heap good dream, 'til Ford be get ahold o' it.' He went on to declare: 'We do seek to establish da community on da basis o' perfect liberty, eco-harmony, 'n da economic justice; da community which, while it do preserve unqualifi'd da right o' e'ery individual to control his or her own actions, do secure to e'ery worker da full 'n uncurtail'd enjoyment o' da fruits o' his or her labor, 'n do make marijuana legal as it do be da natural fruit o' our lands to be use fer our mind-branchin' benefit. Fer da site o' our community we do be give by Da Feds, in gratitude o' our sacrifices in Da War, heap large tract o' land, to be call "Arboretum," in da Oregon territory o' North Usonia with our western border on Da Pacific Ocean where we do be now plannin' our new capital, "Da Clearin'." We do be recognizin' no exclusive right o' property in Arboretum; fer cultivation o' land, as well as fer productive purposes generally, self-suffi-cient groups do be form 'n to maximize da open land fer agriculture 'n forestry, high-rise megastructures call 'top-risers' do be construct'd; each group do share its profits 'mong its members in proportion to their several contributions. Any person do have da right to belong to any association 'n to leave when-e'er he or she do so please.' It is the general opinion, especially among South Californians, that Forester's experiment in woodsy socialism will quickly petrify. Only time can tell. ■

TAR SPACKLED BANNER

In setting forth his *ecological* vision—the hyphen was meant to stress the very *logicality* of Ecozen Gaia peeps *[beliefs]*—Charles Forester waxed eloquent over his proposed eco-experiment, "Arboretum," in a speech made on Earth Day, 2010:

> *I do be seekin' da inheritance all too corruptible, industry-defil'd, 'n that do be fadin' 'way if we be not vigilant—Da Ancient Forests o' North Usonia—which we will be makin' safe from rust (an easy bust) 'n moth (maybe) and da curse o' drippin' acid-rain (small hope). Our birthright do be laid up in eco-heavenly hills 'n do be semi-safe there, to be bestow'd, at da time appoint'd (soon) on 'em that do diligently be seekin' its luxuriance—US nova-citizens o' da pollution free state o' Arboretum. We citizens that, I do be sayin', do be wantin' to be dubb'd 'da branches o' Da Branchland'* [later to be changed to 'Da Branchlando' when Esperanto is forcibly introduced into Arboretum by the Socialist dictator Solan Aceae in 2017 A.D.] *'N we branches to be choosin' da heap appropriate Ecozen logo fer our nova society, Da Moo, be bas'd 'pon da ideogram fer 'Mu' or emptiness—ya peep?* (Forester, *Da Green Book*, 8.)

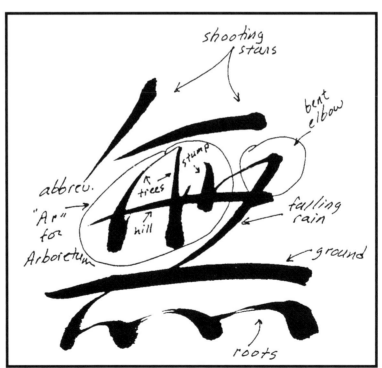

Explanation of "Da Moo," Arboretum's Official Logo

TAR SPACKLED BANNER

C. Forester in Paris (1998)

Forester's anti-80-column-mind ecowritings persistently attackerooed "da stale intellectual tobacco smoke" of acanemia that "do be leavin' da environment out o' peeper [*sight*] 'n cranker [*mind*]," which "do be da clear sign o' evil complicitree [*complicity*] with da destructo-pollutative contracter on da globe that do be 1-sidedly drawn up by purveyors o' pan-capitalism 'n embodi'd in Da Bunker State. Afterall," he said, "who do be askin' Ma Nature if she do be desirin' to be rap'd?" *Moreover*, Forester, sounding even mucho more sour in his bozotic diction and after having studied briefly at the Sorbonne—he called "Da Sore Bun," so painful where the theory lectures—was heap mucho contra that powerful elder-day promoter of the hyperreal, Jean Baudrillard.

Another Forester excerpt:

M. Baudrillard, da heap persifleur *(from* persiflage *meanin' "arrogant mockery") do be seemin' to be 75% rejoicin' that da world o' simulacra do be doin' 'way with what do be seemin' to be da pre-electronic, ol'-fashion'd 'n hopelessly antiquat'd world o' yore. He do seem to be heap oblivious that da computer be not havin' as yet da experience o' crisis o' subjectivitree. By heap contrast, da under-growth* [children] *do be not heap clos'd systems with preprogrammed feedback loops nor be runnin' on socio-autopilot—although da Gen-XXers do be shakin' this my ecofaith on mucho more than 1 occasion, ya peep?*

Da....twang-your-magic-twanger-froggy-'n-be-makin'-materiality-be-gone brand of pessimistic acanemic peep (ho! heap obscenitree) do be not want'd in Our Branchland [Arboretum]. *Da Bunker State, howe'er, do be have Frenchy-friendly commission'd da blarghy abstract, symbolic statue o' this Frog-from-Afar fer da Nova White House—that peculiar pair of tubular tin biggy brackets*

[ ]

facin' each other at exactly da distance 'part as measur'd from shoulder-to-shoulder 'n as tall as da savant *they do be celebratin'. TBS do* idolize *M. Baudrillard 'n do be keepin' da heap o' his peep circulatin' 'mong da masses via da armor'd mobile libraries that persistently prowl da proleborhoods* [working-class neighborhoods]. *We do hope to be establishin' in Our Branchland da place o' mental 'n physical seclusion (be peep'd as* Da Clearin', *da name* o' our capital city) *that do be not subject to da systemic control* (technique *in that Frenchy Jacques Ellul's sense) by destructive orders or strategic configurations. Ergo, we do be fightin' in 'n outside our nova ecotopia da pervasive pan-capitalist ideology of ecodisparagement that do be picturin' da ecological relationship with da world as somethin' heap static (not Gaian), merely uninform'd, passively effeminate, 'n obstructive to business interests. Ya peep? This disparagement do be first broacherooed by 'nother Frenchy, a neo-liberal anti-ecofeminist benam'd Luc Ferry in his blarghy* Da Nova Ecological Order *(1985, reprint in Chicagary, Usonia, 2003). Ferry do be puttin' into 1 category da deep ecologists (Bill Devall 'n Arne Naess), ecofeminists (Val Plumwood 'n Karen J. Warren), 'n differential crankers (Félix Guattari 'n Jacques Derrida) 'n then do be sayin' they all do be havin' heap ties with da fascists (Cormac Da Scald 'n "Monty" Durfuherman) 'n da communists (Solan Aceae 'n Ana Castillo "Jaina" Flores). He be do this 'cause he do note that all 5 o' da grouperoos do advocate raidin'* Lackluster Video *stores 'n be destroyin' da ol' vidtaperoos—*A River Runs Through It *'n* River Wild—*'cause they do be thinly disguiserooed adverts fer selling heaps o' real estate in Montana 'n Wyomin' to CEOs 'n da Globo-Com media stars. Ya peep? Ferry do attackeroo in heaps Guattari's advocatin' da practice o' da art of* dissensus *(da art o' becomin') rather than da neo-liberal notion o'* consensus *(da heap disguise fer globalism as da toutin' o' pan-capitalism as da end o' history). Our Branchland do be da environment's need that be call'd into existence to be startin' da dinky cell o' eco-revival. I, Da Forester, do be only Nature's humble deep ecological servant. Da world do be dynamic 'n creative, not heap passive 'n robot-like. So down with da neo-libs 'n da cyber-sillies; let da branchin' 'n liftin' o' our Branchland be permanent kranchin'. I do declare Arboretum do be da first* post-modem *socius, da only computeroo free-zone in Usonia, nay, in all o' North America! We do be cooperatin' with evolution, da goal-direct'd process that do be not da survival o' da fitest, but da elimination o' da most bozotically competitive 'n ballsy-blarghy individualistic exploiteroos in favor o' those who do be able to cooperate with Gaia's heap cooperative structure 'n thereby be contributin' to da achievement o' Gaia's strategy. Ergo, we do be praisin' da pingful-bubbles* [honored memory] *o' Prof. Christopher D. Stone who do as early as 1972 be broachin' da touchy ecolegal question in da article: "Should Trees Have Standing? Toward Legal Rights for Natural Objects" in* Da California Legal Review. *Ya peep?* (Forester, *Da Green Book*, 10-11.)

TAR SPACKLED BANNER

FROM
DA
GREEN
BOOK

**Charles Forester and wife do the
Log-a-rhythm Dance during the
first anniversary celebration of
the founding of Arboretum (a
stained-glass window in the Civic
Center Complex, Arboretum)**

***Da Heap Forest-Meetin'* (2015)
French artist M. Jean-Marie
Palacios; charcoal depicting the
famous secret meeting between
5 Usonian representatives and
Charles Forester that officially
founded Arboretum in 2011.**

**Cruxifixion of 2 deep
ecologists by surf-nazis**

**Mushot of artist who
was prosecuted by TBS
for his rhizomatic pencil
drawings that were
deemed anti-Usonian**

UTI NON ABUTI

'Da Tres Trees,' Arboretian flag (recto)

Official slogan on the flag (verso)

My Aunt Betty Baskette and note scribbled to my sister: " Dear Brucine, Hope I didn't turn you into a 'basket-case.' Ha-ha! Love, Aunt Betty"

My sister, Brucine, in a deep-ecofeminist art performance at Occidental College

Prof. Stone—some said he had "the X-nature"—urgerooed in the article Forester mentions, "that we give legal rights to forests, oceans, rivers and other so-called natural objects in the environment—indeed to the natural environment as a whole." In contradistinction, Ferry claimed in was heap absurd to grant non-humans rights.

Brucine — my ecologically-minded older sister had lived with our wonky, never-married *[Ellis/Sille used "spinster" here, but Laura balked at its sexism, asking me to replace it with a gender-neutral synonym]* Leaverite Aunt Betty Baskette while attending Occidental College where my other uncle, Neander Storch, was teaching. Boisterous yak-yak over their respective eco-positions would often break out into blarghful blows. Oft incessant arguments about Prof. Stone, Françoise d'Eaubonne *[who coined the term "ecofeminism"],* and Val Plumwood, all who'd had heaps of pingful peepy influence on early 21st-century deep ecology and ecofeminism. My sister, a dedicated member of the Spanglish "Miki Mikiztli Califas—Paz Verde" group and a vehement anti-Leaver, became involved in her senior year in Border Studies with the militant Lesbian eco-feminist group "The Red, Green, 'n Blues" (red for blood, green for ecology, blue for clean water and air). These RGBs polemically attacked the blarghful West Coast surf-nazis—ho! clad in their red and black rubber wetsuits—over their blarghy beach-habits, habits they claimed were "patriotically correct" to wreck havoc on tide-pool, sand and shore. But after after a series of bloody atrocities wrought upon deep ecologists and ecofeminists working along the deter-iorating beaches and sand dunes of Oceano-Pismo Beach *[near San Luis Obispo, California; see image previous page],* the RGBs escalated from mere polemology to fiery eco-terrorist attackeroos. Bru-cine's duties were *in situ* surveillance (she'd been a too-cute "surfer's girl" throughout high school) and overseeing the mixing of their "Mad Meg's Molotov Cocktails" (in college she bartended nights when not involved in various ecofeminist art performances in the area).

Her conception of heaps of pings *[beauty]*, was often debated at Aunt Betty's supper table:

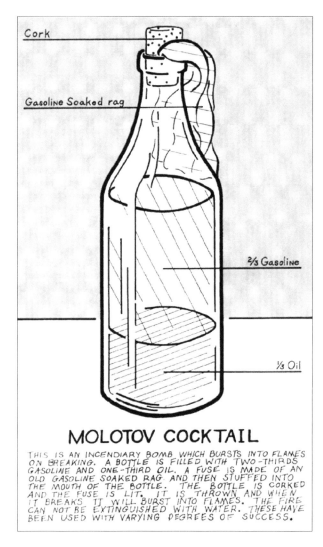

Betty—*heap rétro-clad à la Thrift-Store:* Heaps o' pings? Why Trash Tory *[leader of the Leavers]* in a pile o' nonbiodegradable trash, wearin' his birthday suit, his nude body smear'd wit da heap hodgepodge o' Chile Verde sauce, heaps o' grey poupon mustard, daub o' heap rancid mayonnaise, 'n brown torn plastic grocery bags stuckerooed thereon. Ya peep?

Brucine—*clad in Taco-Bell Birkenstock sandals and an old shredded mu-mu: Nyet*! Heaps of pings is rooted in an aesthetic of nature that guarantees a consciousness of matter that touts heap diversity of species and tongues. Does it matter that life begins in matter? Snatch! Matter is conscious, a *Thing-amabubble* in ecofem terms. As we RGBs chant it:

Life begins in matter. Life is matter. It matters.

Brucine. Ho! A 6-foot 2-inch, eyes of true-blue believer in Reichian Orgone Accumulators; praised diversity up 'n down, side-to-side to the point it became a pingful form of cultimulturalism anchored in her mind-that-matters to bio- and cultural diversity. Produced, she said, pleasure (*ecojouissance*) that, optimistically and contra Baudrillardian technohype, she claimed, "cannot be entirely commodifiderooed by the blarghy Bunker State. Ya peep?"

TAR SPACKLED BANNER

Brucine's Orgone Accumulator

Brucine's Orgone Shooter

Bru'—I always callerooed her that because of her tomboyish habiteroo of always brewing up something weirdly mechanical in poor-put-upon Aunt Betty's 3-car garage—had discovered Wilhelm Reich 1 year after starting menstruation. Ho! Read everything on-line she could grep onto, ya peep? Downloaded loads of planeroos to make her own orgone accumulator and orgone shooter.

Later when her wonky ecofeminism manifested itself, during the West Coast's Great Drought, she began to toyeroo around with mystical Native American Rain Dances and bozotic Reichian Cloudbusters in an attempt to alteroo the blarghy dry clime. "Pingful precipitant precipitation," she wanted.

"Ya don't poke 'round with Ma Nature, Bru'," yelled Aunt Betty over her heap enor-mous plate of Pigs-in-the-Blanket.

Brucine's friend, Karl M_____. with his Reichian Cloudbuster after producing snow in July

"Ya super slow 80-columner!" screamed back Bru', tossing her plate of cabbage-wrapped meatball "piggies" at Betty, 1 errant juice dripping meatball hitting me smackeroo in my nerve-wracked (I was kranching) face.

Ho! A damnbetcha generational clash of tsunamic scale and ferocity washed over them. When the tides retreated, Bru' was to be found off visiting a mail e-mail pen pal she'd been avidly corresponding with on Globo-Com's *alt.eco.orgonon.cum-friend* Usenet. It seems this bearded San Diegan had just completed a Reichian Cloudbuster machine at the Univ. of Calif.—La Jolla and was excitedly experimenting with weather alteration. Once he made it snow in San Diego (see picture).

TAR SPACKLED BANNER

It was this Karl M._____. who convinced Bru' to join The Church of the Ecosafe Green Iguana. It had been Karl's mother who had been the Illustrious High Priestess Egwene, the founder of The Church and The Keeper of the Sacred, Pierced Iguana, Ignose. Bru' said she'd been moved to tears by The Message written in the late-1990s by Egwene, an eco-real estater:

Ignose, The Sacred Iguana

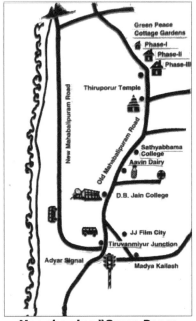

Map showing "Green Peace Cottage Gardens," near Mahabalipuram, India

The Church of the Ecosafe Green Iguana is for all of those Eco-Ig-Green-wanna-bees out there that are trying to do something about the blarghy pollution induced by those pink, hairless apes that are always dumping trash and burning the rain forests. One day the Being of Galactic Eco-Igy-Greeness will come and liberate us. Until that time, we must deal with these prime-time primates as best we can. Come, fellow Iguana-lover, and join us in green peace and hardcore clean up. Maybe even temporarily leave blargy North American pollution behind and buy a lot at our fabulous "Green Peace Cottage Gardens" near Mahabalipuram (40 kms out of Adyar) in beautiful India, where you may enroll for deep ecology classes at D.B. Jain College.

Bru' was nearly signed on the green dotted line to get permanently away from Aunt Betty in faraway India. But she received an urgent letter from uncle Neander touting recently founded Arboretum as *the eco-place* to go. "Heap cooler climate and no monsoons," he said. "Complete sexual freedom for gays and lesbians. Sequoia, Ginkgo, Wolleni pine, but no *ashvatha* trees. And, The World Tree, supposedly an ancient Ginkgo, is rumored to have been found by Charles Forester and his wife somewhere in Arboretum." Bru' bit.

69

TAR SPACKLED BANNER

IV

He who begins by steeping himself in the allegedly self-evident truths of introspection never emerges from them.
　　—Claude Lévi-Strass

Nothing distinguishes me ontologically from a crystal, a plant, an animal, or the order of the world.
　　—Michel Serres

Da fluid-self do be heap like da ever-moving river that do be always flowin' 'n yet do be remain' stable relative to da continual collapse o' its banks 'n da irreversible erosion o' da mountains 'round it, ya peep?
　　—Charles Forester, *Da Green Book*

Charles Forester's ecoself-deprecating *Contamino ergo sum*—"With e'ery exhalation I be do pollutin' da environment, *ergo* I do be constitutin' da *plaque* or da physical *scoria* o' human encrustation 'pon da globe, ya peep?"—did charm my ecoguilt-ridden sister, who was being pursued by homophobic surf-nazis, into immigrating to ecofriendly Arboretum in 2014.

An Arboretian recumbent bike

To Aunt Betty's chagrin and delight, Bru' was repeatedly called to a local plant nursery for interviews. Filled out reams of re-recycled paperwork (glork! yes, all hardcopy, computers being heap *Verboten* in 'Da Branchland'). After stringent ecopsychological examination and accept-ance of her 500-word exegesis of the Zenecological koan: "What is the sound of no pine cones dropping?"—she and Jump-jeterooed northward to her new ecohome to become an Arboretian *nova-branch* (new citizen). But ho, blarghy day! Just 2 months later she was killerooed, her rumbly recumbent bike mysteriously having left the dirt road and kisserooed a lusty Douglas fir head-on while coasting

Brucine's skull after restoration

(what the locals there call *nopin'* in their bozotic Slango) down a steep incline at high speed near the town of Altajo in Da Catkins mountains. The Official Arboretian Extinction Certificate gave, in the snappy hand of the Da Examinin' Forester, the cause of death as:

Nappin' while nopin'.

TAR SPACKLED BANNER

As per her the dictateroos of the ecofeminist RGBs who impugned anything having to do with "cut, lack, and suture," her will instructed that her corpse not be sent to a conventional funeral home. She was brought back home to San Angelo in a horse-drawn logging truck, ripe to be "eco-cleaned" to the bone by a particularly flesh-hungry Amazonian species of maggot in the basement "Eatemortuary" rigged up in the basement of The Church of the Green Iguana. Her bones were then pound to soft white powder for use in various ecofeminist drugs and potions. Ho, hard blargh! Meanwhile, the immediate family was given her skulleroo, as it is heap devalued by the

Simartists create a simhab at the San Angelo Metroland Basin Natural History Museum

ecofems. Perceiverooed to be both the site (mouth and tongue) of the weaning of the child from the mother's breast and wherein the establishment of the patriarchal Symbolic was initiated by Language—ya peep? Due to the blunt trauma it'd sufferooed, her skull had to be extensively repaired by an anthropologist from the San Angelo Metroland Basin Natural History Museum. The very Museum where Bru' and I'd spent insanely great hours perusing the simhabs, *trompe l'oeil* animal habitats employ-ing a heapful hodgepodge of acrylics, I-Max rear projection scrims, HD-video, simsmells, even V-R. We, especially, were drawn to the habitats ringed with "Under Construction" signs:

///UNDER CONSTRUCTION///

It was the only placeroo we could still peeperoo some species of plants and trees that had recently become, as the ecofems figure it, *X-tinct*. I even still have a digi-pic that Brucine took of me at that museum, inside the "Can (Wo)Man Survive?" exhibit as I was absorbing what 1 journalist termed "the hectic message of walls jabbing at you, electronic music jangling nerves, ramps rising and dipping—more like a horrific fun house than a biological cathedral." Lost in the fun-house, there Nature's fangs were not permanently under glass with (Wo)Mankind sitting pretty. Ho, no! The gist of *that* bozotic

TAR SPACKLED BANNER

Heaps of peeps at an exhbition

show was to suggesteroo there may not even *be* any natural history mucho longer—ya peep?

I peeped images of the ultimate traffic jam, a junkyard that never ends, a rush-hour that girdles the globe like Globo-Com's ho-incessant broadcasts, overpopulation, heap pollution with fishes dying in poisoning water, chemical spraying, cities dying in swirls of (wo)manmade gook, areas of optimal ozone-depletion, warning of global warming, fate-driven fatigue-clad militiamen drilling for *Factionism, Clubbism, Putschism,* oh-so-caring corrupt politi-critters, funereal acanemics *[Jean Baudrillard?]*, a mysterious monkey on roller-blades, starving middle-aged CEOs, undernourished suburban babies, ghetto-coke kids being saved by Science only to leaderoo hungry desolate lives behind the *cordon sanitaire* established by large city mayors and enforced by both UrbPolice in their Himmelblau spandex suits and AmPat *[American Patriot]* vigilantes garbed in Urbanflage hunting gear, and lab-coated geneticists experimenting with the first generation of cyborgs that later to evolved into the heap-heap controversial creation of the *humanoids.*

The author as a dinky kideroo attending the "Can (Wo)Man Survive" Exhibition

This hodpod of images was flasherooed on huge split-screens or across large white abstract urban-esque forms and tomblike slabs via powerful computer-run slide projectors. Glork! The peep was hard-grep; the noise, I bubble, was splintering, yet over it I heard the ho-whinny of platituderoos: optimitic and hard-nosed pieties about life on the the T-B Enterprise mining colonies on the Moon and the Turner Teddyland retirement community on Mars and the imperatives of pan-capitalist free enterprise. Bru' claimed the heapaganza *[extreme extravaganza]* to be, I bubble *[recall]*, a commercial hyperooed, bogotified *[bogus]* version combining elder-day *[late-20th-century]* artist Krzysztof Wodiczko's politiwonky slide-projections onto public buildings with the hailing-hyperoo of Edward Steichen's famous 1955 photo-mural exhibition *The Family of Man* at NYC's MoMA *[Museum of Modern Art]*.

Moreover. I do crank that these visits had put heaps of ecofear into Bru' and, maybe, why she later took the Green Path. Maybe why even I later followed her inspiration across the chain-link, concertina-topped fence bordering Arboretum. *O.K.* It just sounderoos mucho pingy when I can so hookeroo you, Dear Peeper, with a sentimental reason for my journey. Signals mellow-drama, ya peep? So I confess. It was out of heap self-interest I made that sojourn to "Da Branchlando" back in 2053. Ho! Because of—I check off my blarghy greeds—

✓ **heap-pure pingeroosity** [*idealistic curiosity*]**;**

✓ **the practical demanderoos to garner material to satisfy that classic academic binary: publish or perish (so I don't end up pushing a grocery cart); and,**

✓ **the pingy spyful spin-offs in terms of hard-info for which the pan-corps** [*multinational corporations*] **and USONIA C.I.A. payeroo heap mucho.**

✓ **the satisfaction of my jealousy for those numerous utopian writers of days of yore, especially elder-day utopist Ernst Callenbach** [*who authored* Ecotopia*, 1975*]**.**

Ex-C.A.S.A. faculty member's grocery cart, Chicagary, Usonia

So you peep, I'm mucho more ted-turneresque than ecofeminesque. *Quod erat demonstrandum.* I was only heap trying to overcomeroo that definitely eerie feeling that, despite my netful inceptness, no one resem-bled me and that I resembled no one. I drop my eyes almost every timeroo I meet anyone off-net. Even made experiments whether I could face a column-80er looking at me. Result? I was the heap perpetual repeat chicken-outer. My Vici-rating .15 and my Agitquotient .9 is subnorm, even for an untenured acanemic. "Hop, skip, 'n missin' a gene," claims my lanky local traum-doc [*Explorer Scouts heap-trained in trauma medicine*], Sven S_____.

It is said *kindly* of Sven, a pimply, ruddy-faced Strictobs Lutheran [*a new, extreme Lutheran sect?*], that you can sharpen your synthwood Hello Kitty pencil in his sphincter muscle to a deadly point. According to Globo-Com's White-Collar Defenso-News anchor, Ho Ho Cho: "It damn sure makee effective office-weaponeroo when deftry handred. If the puncture don't getee 'em, the read-poisoning wirr." It is said Ho can speak perfect English, but management insists he do the *l-for-r* bit, etc. as it raises ratings—glork!—not to mention covertly re-enforcing heap good ol' down-home racismeroo.

I confess. I perpetarry *[perpetually carry]* a heap sharp pencil around School—blargh, how vile it oft seems to have to go to the office—in the stiff-style mimed by close-peeping vids of latterday Pres-hopeful Bob Dole try and maskeroo his blinkin' rage. Keeps high Vici- and Orgone-rated students off my turf and out of my T-B BVDs. Deters ripping reprisals from disgruntled, unsavvy grad students who obtain from their committee the following Departmental Stamp of Distainful Correction on the first draft of their written thesis:

ACHTUNG !

We have corrected your work, basing our, ho! (ab)reactions upon *miracle, mystery,* and *authority*. So, indeed, heed.

—C.A.S.A.-C.L. Grad Fac Rev Com

What is *my* pedagopeep *[pedagogic philosophy]*? What do I say in my grad-sems *[graduate seminars]* when facerooed with bored and mutilated Gen-XXXer physiognomies, pungesters *[young punsters?]* fostered alike by ugliness and fear? Ho! Could be summed up in 7 dictaroos. The first, a twisteroo on that elder-day German writer Heimito von Doderer's heap peepful dictumeroo: *At first you break windows. Then you become a window yourself.* A heap-ho warning re: the bureaucraticization of the imaginative which I give my lickin' gradpups *[brown-nosing graduate students]*, suggesting they that heap reverseroo into a PoMo-strat of *detournment [a 1960s French Situationist term signifying the aesthetic tactic of Postmodernist quotation coupled to an internal critique of that which was appropriated]*:

1) Culturo-quotable:

Be a window first, then put your fist through it.

(Fact: C.A.S.A.-C.L.'s 2050 MFA show's theme was "Broken Windows 2050".)
I also remind them to mine and mind the remaining pet dictaroos of mine.

2) socio-political:

Cultural underdevelopment of, and othercide in, the semiprolepop [part-time employed majority] *are blarghy pan-capitalesque tech-doms* [evil pan-capitalistic techniques of domination] *found heaps-there* [everywhere] *in TBS* [The Bunker State]. *So remember that: 'Stuffing the mort monied monarch into his safe-deposit box is a task for writerly armies of the circumspect.'*

3) socio-pathetic:

How can you be heap alienated without first having been connected? Crank back and heap try and rebubble [recall] *how it once was.*

4) anti-interpellato-strategic:

Don't become Un Cousteau del Corazón [a Jacques Cousteau of the Heart]. *'Going beneath the surface' is TBS's heap* ancien grand métaphore. Ho! *Just peep our pop-built mellow-drama and fed-builts* [popular cultural themes and terrorist-safe federal buildings constructed underground]. Ho! *Describe the outerworld of the innerworld of the outerworld. Ya peep?*

5) exploratoro-parataxic:

Be
grepping
around
admire
lists

6) aesthetico-linguistic:

Do bahuvrihi—*a term designating a compound noun (such as 'bone-head') or a compound adjective. In visual terms: a photograph of a photograph.*

7) psycho-analytic:

Take VOWS; i.e., "Become a victim of wahnsinnige Sehnsucht" (inappropriate longings). *Be like a golden section gone berserko.*

TAR SPACKLED BANNER

Scene: *Combined Art Schools of America—Chicagary Loop campus (C.A.S.A.-C.L.) located in the former State of Illinois Building); first class session of the Fall 2047 semester. I stand arms akimbo in front of my grad-sem in the third-floor classroom #316, sharp Hello Kitty pencil firmly in hand. I wear the mandatory official C.A.S.A.-C.L. International Klein Blue faculty spandex jumpsuit with built-in projectile-proof vest and stand before a*

Department Insignia

sign reading: 'In the Beginning was the Word, then it was the Quote and now it's the Statusquote.' The pointing-digit shoulder-patch I sport indicates my department, Creatidigible Writing, where, as our slogan puts it: "Your digits [typing hands] meet our digits [computers]"). My

Rank Patch

pedastatus, Associate Perennial-Part-Timer, indicated by a running-figure-on-the-classroom's-right-wall chest-patch. Red slashes on the left sleeve shows years of service. Grant awards would decorate the right sleeeve—the more politically-correct conservative faculty members have scores, which they display on a maroon sash like Boy Scout merit badges. Supposedly sound-proof sem-room, but banging neo-Bhangra music heard [Punjabi folk, Bombay film music, and dash of neo-disco]; room painted a graffiti-resistant semi-gloss Navajo White and vid-monitored for security and the Dean's personal peep. The interior ping-clean and geo-sharp, mucho the better to contrast with the disordered detail and vertiginous experience of the bozotic-baroque that constitutes constructed-reality à la midcentury. The felt-tip pen board behind me permits its penned contents to be ho-now Xeroxed for the class with touch of the pedagogical digit. Dandy-ho for subgradpups who: 1) are lazy; or 2) lost an arm or hand in combat; or 3) are functionally illiterate; or 4) can't afford a PowerBook. I stand nonchalantly, sipping a cup of the bitter herbal Brazilian Pau d'arco bark tea, lapping up the lapachol, a supposed homeopathic remedy for the bitter reception my teacherooing gets from the more mucho gumbified gradpups). Start to point out to those gender-boinking Gen-XXXer femino-macho thesistuds— ho! lounging uneasily before me in black synthleather beanbag chairs—the glorky [surprising, startling] gisteroo of Contemp-writ Lit-crit.

Me: Ho! That Frenchie *[Paul]* Valéry once scribbled—I trans-lateroo—'Sometemps I crank that there will be place in the future for a Lit the nature of which will singularly resembleroo that of a sport.' And that sport, I declaim, is now heap peeped as 'Playin' Jarism.' Ungentlemen . . . *[I pause as several male-coded gradpups scratch their real, or simulated, choads (penises)]* ho! starteroo your central processors, *throttle* forward into cyber-spaceroo! And don't bustbubble *[forget]* to wear your 'bullies' *[bullet-proof vests]* for as some departmental wit once writ: 'Unless you're alive you can't play.' Ya peep?

TAR SPACKLED BANNER

Ho! Bubbly *[remember]* that Freud peeped that representation is a 'cannibalistic discourse,' which we must mucho more cannabalize for our pingful politipurps. Ho! Yes, merry thieves us all in our Sherwood Forest of Signs. Robbing the sign-rich for the benefiteroo of the sign-poor. Copping both white-pop and hicult symbols constitutes a kind of refusal, a don't want of the what-was and what-is, an endless gameroo of montage and sabotage even, paradoxically, as it's a polite hats-off to the dead 'n dying.

Idoru Shizumi *(a plonker* [someone who behaves badly], *'Geek-girl' to her admirers; a peeper of the 'aesthetics of disappearance' as she rarely attenderoos class; always P.C., writing 'she' as '$he'; she now spits on her palms and rubs them vigorously, a sign of disdain and says in Japanese):* Ho! *Saru-mane-ya! [Copycat!]*

Dominio "Riflusso Ragione *(An Italianate zipperhead* [closed minded guy] *with a painted face; sits next to 'Geekgirl' whom he perpetually paws; fled Italy to avoid the Bosnian War draft. According to Sir Lento's Attention Curve, he is now at the* asymptote *of attention, having passed the* cliff *and taken the* ride. *Fashion-able, he wears a shredded Bosnian peasant dress—all the rage now since the revelation of the sexual atrocities of the D.N.D.F. (Divided Nations Defense Forces Forces) against Bosnian Serbian civilians—over a black spandex body-stocking. His hefty norm-issue Saucie Aussie-built Bowie-Wowie knife rests ready on his lap; an inscription on its abalone shell handle reads: 'No hope, no fear.' A Sharper Image (made in Hong Kong) jade rape whistle dangles from around his long neck. His samesex mates call him 'a wild boy gone for baroque,' a pungster in Italian and English, an expert in virtual Neo-Conceptual Art and Telepresencing. His made-in-Napoli Testone brand 'trodes, all gleam and glare, barely peek out from under his thick mat of dark hair. No kranching tarnish there! On his terse application statement he listerooed his 'engenderment' as 'at homo doing anything,'* his *'glamorous-precedent' as 'Caravaggio,' and his 'nyet-peeped cranker'* [least-downloaded thinker] *as 'Gianni Vattimo,' that venerable elder-day Italian PoMoish '75 Mhz.-Cranker'* [a late-20th-century proponent of Postmodernist 'Weak Thought'].

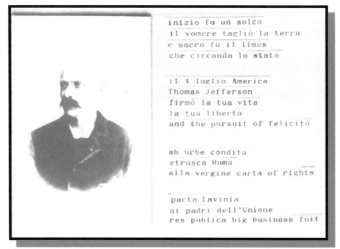

Subgrad work, the "Testamento Di Intenzionalita"
series, Dominio "Ruflusso" Ragione (2048)

Ragione (2052)

Exhibition announcement for "Les Mots Joe,"
a digimugshot series, Dominio Ragione (2051)

TAR SPACKLED BANNER

At C.A.S.A.-C.L., Dominio has run out of zorch [favor] *gaining a blarghy repute as a neo-neoconservative, hiding under false-duds his desire for a dominant, totalizing discourse, a transcendental signifier rooted in Enlightenment Reason, and a 1930ish passion for both D'Annunzio's poetry and Guisseppi Terragni's fascist architecture, etc. (i.e., he's a phoney, what in Arboretum I found out they call a 'paste'). Among the (too few) 'Bros' at C.A.S.A. he was taggerooed 'Da Blarghbot' for being* heap *anti-chip hop (a cybero-hackish version of elder-day hip hop culture whose looping-whooping mantra—'Take dem break 'n repeat it, take dem break 'n repeat it'—was first promulgated by Muhammad Bam Baataa in that textual thicket of spoonerisms titled:* Da Main Festo o' da Digerato, *2045). Raising his nail-painted olive-hued hand, making the Sign of the Cross, he has his* heap *foundationalist objectioneroos to offer to my 'weak thought' with its ontology of declineroo, definitive farewell to reason, and peep* [belief] *in an aesthetics of finitude and quotationism):* Ho, pedder [teacher]! Rifiuto, rifiuto [trash]! Scusi! Preferisco la musica classica e un bel libro! *I thirst for the once unpolluted port of Napoli* [according to Arboretum *an oil tanker disaster ruined the ecology of the Naples port and coastline and heaps of Neapolitans immigrated*], *the returneroo of the*

Neapolitans fleeing a polluted Naples happily arrive in New Yorsey, Usonia

nova, the phallus, and heap peep [complete knowledge], *in the peepless obeds* [blind obedience] *to the all-elbowority* [strong authority] *of the Logos and its ho-heap hegemony of far-peepin'* [dominance of vision]. Capisce?

Me (*I draw a sketchy semblance of a pan-capitalist Globo Monopoly board with my felt-tip pen*): Go heap straight to the middle of modernity, do not pass Go; take a Chance card: read extensively as 'tradition of the error,' go straight to modernist Jail as the paradoxical but ultimate strategy of its own overcoming. After you're paroled *[a pun on the French word* la parole, *meaning 'utterance' or 'speech act' in Saussurean structural linguistics]* go to the nova border world of Greater Sanfebuquerque *[Santa Fe - Albuquerque Metroland Complex],* from Mazdaztlán Motors hire a *faux ancien* metal beast—a powder-blue rétro Mazda Miata—slip a VCD *[very compact disc]* into the stereo and driveroo out along the *bandito*-bugged, *brujo*-lined, Interborderstate into what's left of the Nueva Mexican desert, into the *terreno peligroso* of *Gringostroikalán* [*the heartland of the Southwest's militant grassroots anti-pan-capitalist movement*]. Then *maybe* you'll begin to crank [*think*] transversally, rejecteroo AmPatish *othercide*, and become a heap *borderígena*, a schizzy full-citizen of the nova border world. Ya peep?

Danger zone/Terreno peligroso

[*Whoops at this admonition from the mucho more pedder-lickin' pups, except for 'Geekgirl' who mucho pups peep as heap* nō-nashi, *clueless.*] That will involveroo you, Ragione, in heap-reaching implications: a rad-reval [*radical revaluation*] of 'remaking' and 'rewriting.' Ho! Pup, as 'An Attempter of a Mourning Feelosofy,' I believe in the heap refusal of the idea of a reconciled totality which heap removes the possibility of being heap redeemed. *Moreover. . . [I, unbefullypeeped by the pups, slyly defend my fetishistic, fascinating, albeit illegal, useroo of the Maytag dryer cum time-machine.*] The present no longer defines itself on the basis of its break from the past [*the pups nod their agreement*]; insteaderoo, its links to the past are baserooed on a 'quotationist' attitude [*the pups clap*] which springs from the heap constitutive strengtheroo of bebubbling [*recollection*] at the serviceroo of a subtle internal critique, a

The Taco-Bell PowerBook

weakly *detournment*, of the paltry symbols of our bozotic timeroo [*I take a bow*]. Pups, a critique of these symbols is a critique of our lives [*the pups transcriberoo this wisdom into their PowerBooks*]. Have you, my valid invalid, zippiddy-downloaded my hypercritsay [*hyper-texted critical essay*] "Napoli heap like New Yorsey [*the New Jersey - New York Metroland Complex*]?" If not, plug-in—ya peep?

Ragione (*while smiling, an angel of seeming affability, his index finger of his right hand draws an imaginary line from his left ear across the throat to the right ear*): Ho! Sure, *babbo [dad]*!

TAR SPACKLED BANNER

By the end of the gradsem, Ragione is waxerooing eloquent. 'Geekgirl,' having debubbled [forgotten] her Ritalin, is bouncing in her bean bag chair to some unheard drum solo.

Ragione *(ignoring the horrorific hisses from his fellow pups)*: Humanotsokind is pre-eminently a heap telic-creato-destrutive animal, striverooing consciously and unconsciously toward a goal, perpetual engineers of land, bodies, and minds. Humanotsokind heap neederooes firmly foundations even—ho, especially!—in these days of keep-drifting nomadism. Humanotsokind is heap incessantly roamerooing in heap need of building Roman roads— ho! those veritable lasagnas of durability—wherever they may lead.

Ragione boots up his T-B PowerBook, his wireless modem connecting him to Globo-Com Net's on-line Globopedia Home Page called 'I Crank Icon, I Crank Icon' (the title being a punful play on the quaint optimistic phrase 'I think I can. . . . I think I can.' repeapted by the train in the famous rétro children's book The Little Train That Could).

HO! IT'S GLOBOPEDIA!

I Crank Icon — I Crank Icon

Click on Andy to enter

Our Founder, Dr.   Andy Ure, says:

     Globopedia *is the heap great minister of civilization to the terraqueous globe and the cyperspaceous hypersphere, diffusing the life-blood of science, religion, and ideology to myriads still living in the region and shadow of ignorance. Ya peep?*

Clicks on the 'Andy' icon. The 'Turkish Phood Craze Frase of the Day' globo-cuisine vocabulary builder feature appears:

TÜRK YEMEK/TURKISH FOOD

DENIZ HAYVANLARINDAN NELER VAR?

WHAT KINDS OF SEAFOOD DO YOU HAVE?

_____

Contents **HO! CLICK HERE TO PEEP GLOBOPEDIA**

Ragione clicks on the 'Contents' icon. In seconds, he has accessed 'Rome, ancient, roads' and downloaded a diagram of the 5 layers composing those imposing Roman roads of yore:

LAYERS OF THE ROMAN ROAD

_____ SUMMA CRUSTA

_____ NUCLEUS

_____ RUDENS

_____ STATUMEN

_____ PAVIMENTUM

Heap unlike you *babbo*, we others neederoo all the firmly found-ations for crankin' 'n truckin' *[thinking and becoming]* as we can garneroo. *[Looking heap macho in his war-paint]* Rather than doing 'Uterineroo' feelosofy from 'down-under,' we want to stay on top—ya peep? Toast-Posties *[burnt-out postmodernists]* like you offer sophisticated and persuasive criteroos of foundationalism and essentialism, but your conceptions of social criteroo tend —ho!—to be wholly acanemic.

[Ellis has Ragione espouse a key problem here: the political result of post-modernist theory—with its decentering, deconstructing, and weakening of totalizing narratives—can actually end up de-potentiating the strong narratives of marginalized others, others whom may be just at the threshold of gaining access to the center, to dominant modes of discourse. Hence, the skepticism of many groups such as Latinos, Blacks, First Nations Peoples, etc. toward Postmodernist theory.]

In order to heap peep *[completely understand]* the sourceroo of my de-potentiating propensity for '75 MHz. cranking' *[Postmodernist Weak Thought]* one must turn the clock back for a portrait of this cranky-scribbler *[precocious writer]* when Mother and Father were called 'Mops 'n Pops' and my earliest extant diary entry read:

D.E. 3/15/09

Thanked pingful Pops for My First Komputer. Thanked Mops for not smoking near it.

Ho, story-tempo is now every day: 'Once-a-upon-a-tempo (and a heap pingful tempo it was) a sim-moocow coming down along the virtual path and this sim-moocow that was down along the virtual road met a nicens dinky blargh-boy from Aussieland namerooed Tuckeroo.'

Komfortin' Komputer Game told me that story, a cybersitter that looked at me raster-ishly through the glass with a pixellated face. 'The sim-moocow came down the road where Betty Binny lived in a shoe. A soulful duck, she loved to kranch on Kranch Day. 'All komputer-kinder must kranch on Kranch Day'.' That's what she said ho enough.

'Forget to kranch, get the branch!' That's what this cybersitter says. Cyber-Sabbath—ho hum—can't be on-line or playums VR-version of 'Threshold of the Roji' with its thicky black Niponese kanji lettering as tall you are and all those sad-grey kimono-clad Samuraibulletheads with wraparound shades and shoulders big as a side of Kobe beef who bustle about saying: 'Shita ni! Shita ni!' while 'The Master of Nothingness' lotus sits calming putting incense in a black burner whose grey smoke pixel-twists into mysterious words that hover before him. Like the bozotic feelosofic message: 'Rakan! Peeping all the way into the universe from what lies before you gets you a score of 1000 yellow petals from the Mitsubishi Chrysanthemum.'

But—ho!—mucho more zipperheadedness. On that blarghy Cyber-Sabbath, if you got 'trodes, even just backing up one's crankessenceness wiil get you zorched with the blarghy parental stun-gun.

Mops mad I still wet the bed. Sure sign of abnormally low Vici-rating, Pops says. When you wet the bed, first it is warm then it gets cold. Danger of short-circuit in 'lectric bammy. So now Mops got me an alarmed oilsheet that ring-rings when blarghy damp and then Mops (or Pops) come blowing cigarette smoke and change my sheets.

Sim-Kitty got a nova cybercat upgrade today, she purrs heap pingy now. But Mops doesn't like the nova sim-shit feature.

TAR SPACKLED BANNER

[Ellis here travesties the beginning of that famous "lying autobiography," James Joyce's The Portrait of the Artist as a Young Man. *But, unlike Joyce, Ellis would have us believe he—a four years old at the time, 'a precocious Komputer-kinder'—could write such a diary entry. 'Shita na!' ('Bow down!') is an expression often used in Japanese* chambara *movies, while 'Rakan' is Japanese slang for 'skin and bones Buddhist fanatics.']*

Mops and Pops' Pops 'n Mops were born born (both) in Elderon, Wisconsin. Ho! A town with a nameroo heap wonky enough to make it into a Kurt Vonnegut novel. Grandy-Pops was Grandy-Mops' elder by 2 years, but since she outlived him by 2 years, they died even-steven. My Grandy-Pops breached the day the Russians put Sputnik in orbit. Grandy-Mops saw first light the night those Rock 'n Roll singers had their peepholes closed after diving into a frozen Iowa corn field. They each learnerooed to chain-smoke-smoke at Guth's, a local farmers' bar with heaps of dead animals on knotty pine walls and passerooed the skills down to their children. My Mops and Pops, always reeking of cigarette smoke, sniffed each other out in high school at The First Annual Elderon High Disco Prom. Ditched their Prom dates to go park out at Grabass Lake they did where, my Mops later allegorically confessed, winking: "I smoked your father's corncob pipe and got ashes on his polyester bell-bottom pants." After graduation they married. They moved to Green Bay for college, then to Chicagary (it was still 'Chicago' then) where Pops sold Westinghouse elevators; there they had Bru' and mucho later me. Pops later relocated us to San Angelo (Los Angeles at the time) on a get-rich schemeroo to sell GM's Impact EV nova electric-powered automobiles to smog-choked Angelinos, while making discrete Internet inquires to Crete about introducing that model to Greek and Turkish markets countries eager for the nova technocars after the infamous Athens and Istanbul respirasters *[hundreds of respiratory failures, smog-related deaths?]*. I bubble *[remember]* Pops puffing foul-smelling, hand-rollerood Turkish cigs and studying his Berlitz *Turkish Phrase Book and Dictionary*. Ho! Even reciting out loud funny-sounding phraseroos like:

Nerededir bar?	*Where's the bar?*
Bir paket sigara, lüften.	*A packet of cigarettes, please.*
Nargile istiyorum.	*I'd like a hubble-bubble pipe.*
En yakin tütün saticisi nerededir?	*Where's the nearest tobacconist's?*
Işte bir küçük sağlam elektrik araba.	*Here's a small sturdy electric car.*

Pops argued that with air-pollution down in the various metropolises, tobacco-smoking might catch on again, people using the cleaner air as a rationalization for another cig or more per day. He pitcherooed this concept

TAR SPACKLED BANNER

GM's Impact EV Car and Logo

to the International Tobacco Lobby. Got heaps of undiscloserooed amounts of "donations" to GM's globo-advert campaign which got him the heap privilege of designing GM's nova logo which was so ping-perfect it won him a first place trophy in LogoCentric's Annual Design Awards which got him invited by the Turkish government on an all-expenses paid trip to Ankara, Turkey to further discuss the use of "green cars" in that country. This was 4 years prior to the Bosnian invasion of Turkey, 5 years prior to Don-de-bartender's blarghy demise near Edirne.

Pops gave a heap energetic talk to the governmental gumbies in the Transportation Department. The next day he asked where he might buyeroo a Turkish-English-language newspaper—"*Nereden bir Türkçe-Ingilizce gazete satin alabilirim?*"—so he could read the response to his presentation. He was surprised to find a heap detailed description of his *presence* during his presentation but heap dinky info about the *contents* of his presentation. Pops had kept the newsclipping:

> . . . a handsome man, unlike most Usonians in being gentlemanly in his manner and attire; 6 feet and better in height; his chewing gum ineffectively masked his smoker's breath. His lips were delicately thin and receding and this seemed to be natural and not due to surgery; his teeth were tobacco-stained. . . . His eyes were blue or light grey (his ozone-protector glasses prevented this reporter from being more precise here) and not very clear nor quick, but rather heavy (maybe due to jet lag); except as I had opportunities for observing when he was excited in his public presentation over 'green cars' and ecological issues; at which times they seemed to distend and protrude; and if he worked himself furious, they became heap blood-streaked, and almost started from their sockets. Then it was that the expression of his lips was to be observed—the kind smile was exchanged for the curl of eco-scorn, or the curse of eco-indignation at air-pollution. His voice was bellowing; his face swollen and flushed; his griped hand beat as if it were to pulverise coffee beans for Turkish coffee; and his heap whole manner gave token of a painful energy, struggling for utterance over 'the need to treat the environment and people in it ecoally.'

TAR SPACKLED BANNER

Hilton Hotel, Ankara, Turkey

Ho! Pops so surprised by the words of this correspondent—as per his after-yak to us upon returning—his mouth opened a centimeter too too far. The *akide şekeri* (candy) he was so-sucking on in an attempt to chain-saw his chain-smoking, in betwixt slow sippies of local plonker *[heap cheap booze]*, fell and bumblarghy-bounced once, then again, on a "Tapis de Rabat," the light-green Oriental rug (see image on left) placed heap neat on his Hilton hotel room floor. So he was forced to *disconfect* it, sterilizing the pink candy by—ho!—blowing on it, assuming this would somehow really remove all the blarghy germeroos.

Poor Pops. He didn't bubble *[remember]* the facteroo that ideas of instability, of fluctuation, are, *moreover, a threat* as well as a hope. Small fluctuations—like blowing off candy—may grow and change the overall structure of stuff. Pro is that individual activity is not doomerooed to insignificance, con is that this is also a threat, as our blarghy universe has seemed to have lost the security of stableroo, permanent rules—gone forever. We are living in a wonky wide-world that inspires no blind confidence in those with peepers *[eyes]*, and no insightful confidence in those without. At the heap pingfulest, we can perhaps only legitimately harbor a feeling of what our President Bezilius "Coach" Windrip heap aptly, heap eloquently, calls "qualified hope." What our Gen-XXX teeneroos dub "Chicago Hope" after the touch 'n go emergency-room scenarios of the rétro-TV program by the same name. Ya peep?

TAR SPACKLED BANNER

As for his "green car" project, Pops' qualified hope turned into bumblarghy despondency. Ho! Whether it was due to dropping that sticky piece of candy or not, we'll never bepeep, but for 4 days Pops couldn't leave his Hilton hotel room. Some obscure Muslim sect emerged from dusty, narrow streets to protest the electric car as heap blasphemous and, *moreover*, blarghy dangerous when used around a worshipful populace ever-immersed in water purification rites. English-language newspapers were soon running headlines such as:

A Usonian businessman in the Hilton is up to the hilt in menacing Muslimic personages

and

Muslim sect pulls plug on electrifying plans of visiting Usonian businessman

and

Discouraged Usonian reportedly sits staring for hours at his own bedraggled image in a mirror

Pops' *Self-Portrait in a Mirror, Ankara*

The latter headline misinterpretes an innocent fascination. Heap struck by the journalist's description of him during his presentation, Pops used his idle time to mercilessly explore his own visage. He persistently sketched, erased, and resketched his self-portrait in the mirror in his hotel room *cum* prison. Had learned something of the manual skill needed by peeping old contra-computer rétro-reruns of Mr. Nagy's "Learn to Draw" TV programs way back when. Ho! What a peeptacle: Inside Pops wore his only pencil down to a dull nub, outside the black-veiled protestors sharped their unpingfulish pikes.

Brucine (left) in her rétro duds with Aunt Betty Baskette at Cincinnati's famed Oktoberfest at the Hofbrauhaus Outpost (Digi-pic by my father, 2010)

Ho! Pops saved by a bloody massacre! Heap pissed Armenian Separatists attacked a Turkish *Câmi*, a mosque, in Kars with a bomb. Seventy-three peepholes heap-fast closed in 37 seconds. Small revenge for thousands killed by Turks earlier. *Ergo*, another objecteroo for popular rage. The peaked pikes veered toward the Armenian ghetto for mucho more fare. Pops was no longer so unpop with the populace. So Pops popped his head outdoors and was able to peeky-sneak out of his hotel, back-alley back out of Ankara, jammed his way onto a Jump-jeteroo and up 'n away'd it from Turkey to Tirana, Albania. There Pops hopped an armored troop train filled with Divided Nation Defense Forces to Munich, Weiterdeutschland (Wider-Germany created under their beloved Chancellor Chaot U. Tintenpisser III during his *almost* bloodless economic *Blitzkrieg* against the European Union in 2005 - 2008). In Munich he visited the revered grave of Russian refugee Timofej Prochorov, the famous "Hermit of Oberwiesenfeld." He thanked his Lord for his safe delivery from the Islamic hordes at that long-lived Hermit's hand-built Ost-West Friedenskirche (East-West Peace Church) on a plot of sacred earth on the Olympiagelände. He marveled at this improvised oil-barrel-domed chapel built after the Blessed Virgin's personal request for a holy site dedicated to post-war reconciliation. Then Pops flew direct on Taco Bell Delta Airlines to Munich's Sister City, Cincinnati, Ohio. Ho! There, appropriately, he met up with my sister, Bru', and Aunt Betty Baskette. They were on a brief Midwestern vacation to pingy *[enjoy]* a boozy *Oktoberfest* with Bru's girlfriend's family (the Grossherzig's) at Cincinnati's heap pop sim of the Bavarian capital's original Hofbrauhaus. In keeping with the frayed frontier spirit of a now-faded Ohio, the local burghers insisted they name it:

𝕳𝖔𝖋𝖇𝖗𝖆𝖚𝖍𝖆𝖚𝖘 𝕺𝖚𝖙𝖕𝖔𝖘𝖙

Poor discouraged Pops. Popping St. John's Wort to enhance his mood, downing steins of *Okotberfestbier* to forget his failure. Upon his return to San

Pops in his 1951 Studebaker which he converted to electric-power drive

Angelo, he took his mind off his troubles by a) doing the virtual Stations of the Cross; b) limiting his electric car sales to San Angelinos; c) buying and restoring an ancient 1951 Studebaker convertible, converterooing it to run efficiently and oh so slickly and silently on ho-fresh

ELECTRIC BATTERIES

hidden in the ample trunk. Ho! Did Pops love the front "spinner" on that car! A pointed device reminiscent of those pointy brasseries so heap pop with women in the 1950s.

But it wasn't until Pops put his résumé in at Fuzzy Logic Unlimited—a

Fuzzy Logic Unlimited Headquarters, San Angelo Metroland Basin

Japanese-based electronics firm that had installed the first fuzzy-logic subway in Sendai in northern Japan way back in 1987—that his life took even less focus. Mops used to observe an inverse proportional relationship at work here: "As our society's blarghy future becomes clearer, your Dad's just gets fuzzier!" Its Usonian headquarters was located on the grounds of the old Anaheim Disneyland site. Ho! Pops was brought in to assist sales development of their new "Fuzzicar," an electric car that manu-

Fuzzy Logic's Corporate Logo

vered itself by following simple verbal instructions from its driver and, with its sensors, could even stop itself when an obstacle was placed immediately ahead. It could be set to react defensively to a car-jacking threat when approached within 1 meter by a blarghy recidivist with a surgically-implanted sub-cutaneous digi-chip Warnroo-Rapsheet.

TAR SPACKLED BANNER

However. Too young to drive, I took mucho more interest in Fuzzy Logic's fuzzy washing machine and dryer set sold under the prestigious Maytag label. Just load in the clothes, press start, and the machine churns, auto-fuzzimagically choosing the best cycle for your load. As you might have already guesserooed, this digression on my Pops was simply to get to this dinky, but signficant, bit of info: It was this exact model of fuzzy-dryer that I later modified into the wonky time machineroo I christened *The Tempo-Tantrum*. But—ho! Dear Peeper—bet you're wonderooing just what bozotic exotic *fuzzy logic* is. **Whaaaaalllll pardner, according to**

Fuzzy Logic is . . .

where truth values are real values in the closed interval [0 . . 1]. This is called a "Fuzzy Set" and it is a superset of of Boolean logic. The definitions of the Boolean operators are extended to fit this continuous domain. By avoiding discrete truth-values, Fuzzy Logic avoids some of the problems inherent in either/or judgments and yields natural interpretations of utterances like "heap hot." The importance of Fuzzy Logic, propounded by Lofti Zadeh from the University of California in 1965, derives from the fact that most modes of human reasoning and common sense are approximate in nature.

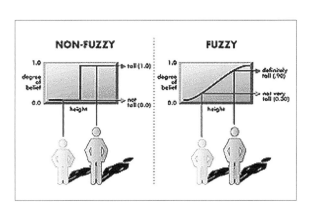

and its essential characteristics are:

- In fuzzy logic, exact reasoning is viewed as a limiting case of approximate reasoning.

- In fuzzy logic, everything is a matter of degree; the Law of the Excluded Middle doesn't apply.

TAR SPACKLED BANNER

■ In fuzzy logic, knowledge is interpreted as a collection of elastic or fuzzy constraints on a collection of variables; fuzzy logic tries to be human.

■ Inference is viewed as a process of propagation of elastic constraints; this is why all Fuzzy Logic employees are required to wear suspenders, not belts.

■ According to Bart Kosko's Fuzzy Approximation Theorem (FAT), a finite number of patches can cover a curve as seen in the figure below. Fuzzy rules define fuzzy patches; if the patches are large, then the rules are sloppy, the smaller the patches, the crisper the rules; Pops was amazerooed how this figure graphically described his famous "5 Martini-Weave" when behind the wheel of his beloved zippy-zappy Studebaker after an afternoon of conviviality with his battery-buddies in the Greater Norwalk Electric Rétro-Car Club:

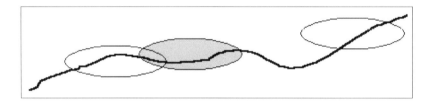

Pops' employment with Fuzzy Logic was heap dinky brief. Due to my youth, the preciseroo circumstance of his demotion, then termination in late 2011, is remains fuzzy, except that his chain-smoking surpassed Mops'. Later I found this confession dated 15 March 2011 when I went through his papers after his death. It may throw light why Fuzzy Logic Unlimited didn't fulfill my father's employment fancies:

> *I spend a lot of my time hoping for some kind of order, some heap hedge against chaos. Some system of authority that will watch over us, and make sure the irrational doesn't get heap out of hand. . . . Some deep part of us seems to need an oversized authority, a faceless guardian who can protect us from our fears. For some it's called state whether it be The Bunker State or the Nova Republik of Texas; for some its the business world whether it be Taco Bell International or its nemesis like the Enochs (see below); for others it's a utopian experiment like Forester's Arboretum. As for myself, it's the battery—Electricity—where the current's either ON or OFF.*

92

TAR SPACKLED BANNER

It was about this time—when I was still dinky, we still lived in San Angelo, and Pops was still commuting to Fuzzy Logic Unlimited in his old electric Stude on the triple-decker Anaheim Freeway—that I had the following horridream. It didn't feel like a dream at all. Ho, no! But like that abused thing: *reality—clear, sharp, unpixellated*. This should tell you a lot about my feelings of insecurity during a time when our cyberopsychic world was filled with violent images from hell-fire, Revelation, and sex; while our real world was filled with live-fire, poverty, oppression, and emasculation. It went thus:

Ho! Trying to sleep on my tummy-tum-tum. But then I must have fallen asleep, yet it seemed what happened seemed a real waking experience. The growl of a tiger. I feel it climb on the beddy-bed and settle its large, warm, fuzzy body down on top of me. Ho! It's heap heavy and breathes. It kneads its biggy claws. I know if I stir or even simply inhale, it will teareroo me to shreds with its sharpy claws. I imagine what it's like to become human huevos rancheros served up on a white sheet. The beast waits motionless, still kneading. Finally, I feel it lift off, or maybe simply slowly dissolve. I awake with a mixed feeling of relief and dread.

What makes the incidenteroo so bozotic and bletch-blarghful is that it seemed so *virtually actual or actually virtual*, not like my norm noncyberdream-eroos which I can now-'n-for easepeep [*always easily discern*] after waking as sheer mere fancy. *Ho! Not this baby though!* I shat thin gruel like Vonnegut's Billy Pilgrim the remainder of the day in betwixt reciterooing the obscure-in-the-extreme dream over and over for my amazerooed mates. They could only toss up their titanium prosthetics or pong their copper 'trodes, claiming heap-ho octal-forty [*they drew a blank*]. Except for "Blarghy Biff," the class's Born-Again Nova-Catholic suffering from spinabifida.

Scene: *Schoolyard, St. Gabriel of the Sorrowful Mother (known for his obedience, charity, and submission) Parish School, Norwalk, San Angelo Metroland Basin. Biff—a digiscan scapular medal around his neck, his wrists tattooed with Rosary beads, 10 per wrist—queries of me.*

Biff: You had your dream yesterday, on September 30th?
Me: Ho, yes.
Biff: Plinko! St. Jerome's heap feasteroo day.
Me: So whateroo, Biff? I didn't eat the cafeteria food yesterday.
Biff: Jerome's sacred emblem is the ho-heap lion.
Me: But it was a *tiger*, Biff! Maybe even sabre-toothed!
Biff: All the same pixels, buckeroo.

TAR SPACKLED BANNER

It's been time equals minus infinity *[a long time]* since I've had had such a drastic dreamly disturberoo. Ho!—now that I crank of it—been time equals minus infinity since Blarghy Biff's Pop's clothiers' blarghy sweat-shop of underpaid and otherwise abused Hassidic Jews was busterooed into splinters and pissed on by a band of iron sledge-wielding Luddish "Enochs" crying *en masse:* "Enoch has financed them, Enoch shall busticate them." These famerooed assaults-from-below, i.e., from a populace of poor, disaffected, semi-enslaved Israelaborites, were mucho celebrated in rad e-zines and in popcant of the day:

TBS SWAT guard against Enochs attacks, San Angelo

The Tattle Tailor's Song

'N night by night when all is still,
'N the moon is hid behind the hill,
When we in Schnapps up to the gill,
We forward march to do our will
With sledge, pissy-hike and fun.
Ho! These proper *Mensch* are for me,
Who with lusty stroke do bespoke
How broke our brothers be.
Great Enoch shall lead the mini-van.
Stop him who dare, who can!
Press forward e'ery gallant guy
With sledge, pissy-hike and fun.

Ho! In junior-high I did a 2.1 MB disk on these rad-remarkable Luddish "Enochs." They had a beyond-gumby recog-code *[not easily broken recognition code]* for their hammer-carrying members:

You must raiseroo your right hand over your right eye.
If there be another Enoch in company he will raiseroo his left hand
        over his left eye.
Then you must raiseroo the forefinger of your right hand to the right
        side of your mouth.
The other will raise the dinky finger of his left hand to the left side
        of his mouth and will yak: 'What are you?'
The answer: 'Oi! Determinerooed.'
He will yak: 'What for?'
Your answer: 'Ho! Minwage *[minimum wage]* and payvac *[paid*
        vacations].'

(*Globopedia*, hyperlink 5003.1)

TAR SPACKLED BANNER

My VE (virtual education) was virtually enhanced by the fast-hum of me-o-mine nova discoverooed psychic energy—that of the dinky, skinny precocious and compulsive, yet uneven and labored, autocyberdidacteroo. What elder-day prophets of doom would have diagnosed as: *Prosthesis disease, death by wiring.* As I jacked into the Net I'd mutter enthusiastically: "I crank icon, I crank icon!" I must have clicked on Globopedia's Dr. Andy Ure icon (see page 81) a heap of sagans *[billion and billions of times]*, downloading an occasional hostile hacker-ooed phrase supered onto the webpage, stuff like:

You're not paranoid, they really are *watching you.*

and

Welcome to Cyberia—where you inmates can build your own prison!

and

Free! Download the new self-helperoo hypertext:
"Komputers, Social Anomie, and You."

and the Chinese cookie fortune-like saying:

Web makes head @-trophy.

Once I discoverooed that the heap same Armenian terrorist group that indirectly got Pops releaserooed from his hotel-prison had hacked a biggy, managing to rig a global search/substitution so that every time the word "Turkey" came up on the Net, the word 'genocide' would be substituted. I peeped this heap good when I clicked on my bookmark for "CyberGranny's Turkey Dinner 'n Trimmin's Recipes" webcyte to surprise Mops with a nova idearoo for the approaching Thanksgiving feast. Ho! Everywhere "turkey" was supposed to be listed, "genocide" appeared instead:

*Have your friends over a real exotic **genocide** feast this year!*

and

*Good **genocide** dressing made easy.*

But ho! Then 1 dreadful drippy day in Chicagary (we moved there after Pops' popped his being fired on us) I zippy-zippy downloaded Nathaniel Hawthorne's— *maybe* it wasn't Hawthorne's, my bubbles *[memory]* as well as my logic is fuzzy—wiggy-wonky so-so short story, "The Horla" from Globo-Com's www.short-horror/startling/~old text. htm. Heard it digitellus *[speak in digital sound]* of a mysterious, horrible, life-sucking night-critter, a *succubus*, that climberoos on top of, and rubby-wrestles with, the startled sleeper. Ho! Was my blarghy night-visitor heap such? Curious, I did a Globo-Com Net Search under "succubus-picture" and retrieved the famous painting on the topic by Henry Fuseli. Reverseroo the sexes of the

The Nightmare, **Henry Fuseli**
(o/c, circa 1780-90, detail)

95

depicted figures so that the succubus is *female* and the victim *male* (as the original myth states) and—horrors!—it was heap like what I had experienc-erooed that blarghy night. Or keep the reverserooed genders of Fuseli's image intact and heap peep as an allegory for TBS's psychoperpetual-motion desiring machine, i.e., its manipulation of the erotics of the dialectic or agon between fear/desire, dystopia/utopia with which it controls our 80-columners *[weak-minded populace]*:

SUCCUBUS (MALE) = THE BUNKER STATE'S
ALL-ELBOWS APPROACH TO REPRESSING DESIRE
ON TOP OF
SLEEPER (FEMALE) THE MARKETPLACE SWOON ENCOURAGING DESIRE

TBS also maintains it's power, its zorch, by *paradoxically* holding out our amazerooing technostuff as *both* friendly and human *and* something uncanny, inhuman, beyond nature. Heap appeals to the docile social subject 's fuzzy logic! Technostuff as located somewhere between 0 and 1.

Not the case for TBS itself! Ho no. It desires its social "zeros" and "ones" sharply focused, preferably on survidcams *[video surveillance cameras]*. That's why Usonia's Department of Sociomedia's official logo/motto is:

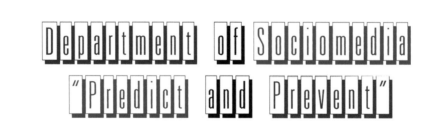

This natpeepcranktankeroo *[national spy/think-tank]* does not have the following terms in its heap gumbified lexicon—missing, missing:

fun
gumby
bogotify
80-columner
wonky (bozotic)
the Aussie suffix *-eroo*

TAR SPACKLED BANNER

Annually, DSM publishes on its webcyte what it deemeroos significant surveillance fare from the past year. Here, Dear Peeper, a dinky sampling:

"Night at the Racists" (right) anti-fascist protest rally results in injuries to both factions. Anti-fascist (left) bleeds RED blood; thanks to this digi-pic, she was later identified, arrested and charged for assault and battery by The Windrip Commission investigating disaffected Commies and anti-fascist terrorism in Usonia.

C.A.S.A.-C.L. art studio faculty caught attempting to suppress laughter during the School President's Commencement Address; thanks to this digi-pic, they were identified and demoted to teaching in the First Year Program at their Chicagary Loop campus in North Usonia

National Artist's Desistance Check is received by an artist who agrees not to exhibit his art on or off the Net

TAR SPACKLED BANNER

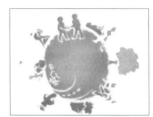

Celebration's Flag

***Perpetual Greenlight*,
sculpture installation,
Celebration, Florida**

This natpeepcranktankeroo, Sociomedia, was the blarghy out-growth of the need to techno-manage Celebration, the privatopia *[planned community]* built by Disney Corp near Orlando, Florida ho-way backeroo in the mid-1990s. *Moreover.* In turn, Celebration, was predicated on Disney's Disneyfied utopia, EPCOT (Experimental Prototype Community of Tomorrow). A nova traditional futurcom designed on 'puter-screeneroos, Celebration was built with a pingpeeper *[keen eye]* toward the elegance of stuff past and near bustbubbled *[forgotten]*. In front of Celebration's Civic Center Neo-Conceptual artist Hans Orlt, installed his famous interactive sculpture *Perpetual Greenlight: Ode to Optimism.* Ho! The mallcrawlers inhabiting there find their (s)mall town crib heap rétrocomfifitted by their corporate parents. As *Globopedia*'s entry on the topic puts it:

> . . . *'The Land Where the Sun Always Shines' was the first privatopia to fully realize the infantilizing dream of the then young theme-park politico and yak-show host, Berzilius Windrip. This was, of course, years before he became our beloved President of Usonia and took the heap beloved tag "Coach" Windrip that his fan club ("The Coach Potatoes") gave him, and some 15 years after the bloody Postal Wars when it was Zip Code against Zip Code with zip-guns—and letter-bombs. Young Windrip, a master punster who can sense the masses' needs like every successful politician before him, said to a real-applauding flesh-audience in William Gibson Hall in the Department of Nova-Prosthetics & Gerontology at the University of McWorld, Silicon Valley, North Usonia during one of his heap rare fleshy appearances off the Net on October 10, 2032:*

>> *'Disney World Realty is a governmental reality, a theme park rah-rah-rah vaulted into a polity with kids as citizens and citizens as kids. So, ho! Aint Government a borin' job 'n best left to the* groanups *[Windrip's own pun here]—those loyal, ho-happy, mouse-loving handful of Disney W.R. (wo)managers?'*
>> (*Globopedia*, hyperlink 1330.2)

Ho! So Celebration set the authoritative standard of *predict and prevent*. Aunt Betty Baskette used to rave about it—had an old friend from high school who married a gumbified corporatcritter, a CEO for Taco Bell Nike who now have the contract for sagans of air-cushion combat boots for both the Divided Nations Forces and the Serbs, the major opponents in the Greater Bosnian Conflict. Betty visited them once. Heaps of pingful stories she told about Celebration, tempered by heaps of blarghy stuff about her friend's husband, Duke "Swoosh" Stump who always said dinky, except for the Gen-X ejaculation—"Cool."

Hailing originally from Meddybemps Grove near Meddybemps Lake in what was formerly eastern Louisiana near Calais, Duke was named after the notorious elder-day fascicritter David Duke. He spent mucho of his kideroo days in a Joe Paterno Day Center in Calais where his mother worked behind 2-way mirrors all day spotting shoplifters and spying on employees at a Nike Shoe Store. He remarked about his own Mops to Betty: "She was considered the eyes and ears of her company." And she liked, admitted Duke, "Being like the Peepers of God which could forever rule out the surprise, the accident, the eruption of the unforpeeped." Ho! The problem of security haunts our blarghy socius and has heaps ago replaceerooed the problem of

"Coach" Windrip on the campaign trail

liberty. *[Ellis paraphrases Jean Baudrillard here.]* Duke was a scholar of Consumofeelsofinosophy and an innovator of Marcosian epistemology, changing Emelda's Cogito, "I shop therefore I am," into the corporatofeel phraseroo: "We shop therefore we are." Yes, Duke was the first to sense the trenderoo away from the elder-day belief that "individuality sells, like sex or Patriotism" toward a mucho more gumbified Corporate We-ism. A We-ism that began with AmPatist *semper fi* and reached its zenith with Berzilius "Coach" Windrip's election to the Presidency in 2052, a victory largely due to his campaign's use of the We-est self-congratulist jingleroo written by "Swoosh" and put on bumper stickers and Globo-Com Net politi-ads:

WE LIKE THE SPRITE IN US
WIN WITH WINDRIP

TAR SPACKLED BANNER

An experteroo in interactive consumerism. Back in the early 21st century "Swoosh" made the cover of *Business Week*. He was responsibleroo for the Tattooed Teen Ear Craze that swept the country. Ho! Sagans of Gen-XX's ultra-modern primitives rushing to have corporate logos pricked into their earlobes. Ten years later, when Betty visited Celebration, he'd just finished the last set of links in what was to become a pingfulest-netseller hypertexteroo *The Niche Marketer's Gaze.*

Terrified mallcrawlers flee Celebration's Post Office after a bomb scare during the infamous Zip Code Wars of 2015

As I said, Aunt Betty liked Celebration, both the town and the act of. "Immune to activist memes," she claimed of that privatopia. That's Betty, a long-time secretary in the 'puter data-entry pool at STRICOM-DNDF (Simulation, Training, and Instrumentation Command—Divided Nations Defense Force) facility in El Segundo *[California]*, she picked up on the jargoneroo. Ho! But not immune to real bullets and explosives as peeped during the blarghy Postal Wars; then it became painfully obvious that everything is simulation but war. *Nevertheless.* Planned leisure communities were fasteroo becoming the norm and, as 1 controversial cranker *[thinker]* saw it, "A certain level of crimeroo is heap part of the necessary roughage of life. Total security only constipates." Like dead, disgruntled Uncle Eustace observes—to the time of "Under the Bamboo Tree"—from some metaphysical limbo in Aldous Huxley's bozotic 1944 novel *Time Must Have a Stop*:

> *Probably constip,*
> *Probably constip,*
> *Probably constipaysh;*
> *Probably const,*
> *Probably const,*
> *Probably constipay, pay, pay . . .*

Mucho members of the still-employed or gainfully-retired heap willfully succumbed to that "Imagineered" (copyrighted term) predictability during the first halferoo of the 21st century. A Lit-critic once celebrated Celebration as *"Our Town* minus the angst," another wonky wit as "Bedford Falls on Prozac." Ho! Celebration was something to celebrate all right.

Not residerooing in Southern Usonia's premier privatopia, Aunt Betty had to take her Prozac orally. Ho-happy though. All STRICOM employees received their prescribed dosages *gratis*—in fact were *requirerooed* to take the stuff. The weekly Dosage Day, as Betty described it, always took place in an enormous oval room on the ground floor with the hyberbolically-curved windows pointing toward the north. One of those curious hermetically-sealed corporate rooms done by some architect, rumored to have once apprenticed under ultra-modernist architect Neil M. Denari, that was too cold in the summer and too hot in the winter. On a typical San Angelo smogday, a harsh thin light glarerooed through the windows, hungrily seekerooing some lab-coated White, or a jump-suited Grey, or even a 3-piece-suited Black. The south-wing of STRICOM housed formidable array of of defense-in-depth receptionists, followed by multiple mazes of cubicles (where Betty worked), and a sun-dial atrium that looked like a nuclear cooling tower.

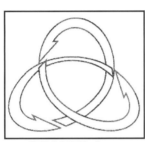

STRICOM's logo

Aunt Betty was 1 of 200 Greys. The doctors dispensing the pills were Whites. Betty's boss and his boss and his boss and his boss were Blacks. The light was frozen, dead, a ghost. Four rows of collapsible white synth-wood tables lined the room, white plastic folding chairs on 1 side of the tables were occupied by the attending medical stafferoo. Four long lines of quiet, docile Bunker State employees fed into the pill-dispensing assembly-line. Pill dispensing, the only activity at STRICOM that wasn't pure post-Fordist. Praise Ford! The doctor whose dispensing line Betty and her *mestizo* workmatey, "Mucha" Malinche, usually rushed to stand in was tall and rather thin but upright with a long chin and big rather prominent teeth, floridly curved lips; his lab-coated

sporterooed a large rétro yellow smile button. *[Ellis travesties the opening lines of Aldous Huxley's* Brave New World *here.]* Like Aunt Betty, he was infamous for his serial monogamy. His age was heap indeterminate—Betty yakked *[said]* 35, Malinche cranked *[thought]* 50—common among these corporate physicians and the managerial staff who had free and frequent (read *requirerooed*) access to plastic surgery—an *enforced* job perk, ho! what in slangeroo is even now called a "jerk-a-perk," or simply a "jap." The ho-higheroo you went up the Corporate-We ladder, the mucho more "japs" you got.

Betty and Malinche fed dataroo into the military-entertainment industry's huge Taco Bell Onyx10 housed far underground that createrooedd the famous STOW (Simulated Theaters of War) where "all the Divided Nations' services play together" and, through SIMNET, fed networkrooed computer simulations to several theme parks in San Angelo. It had a memory capacity of 1280 GB, memory bandwidth of 40,000 MB/sec/CPU and, most importantly for simulation graphics, the capability to generate 100K polygons at 300HZ/pipeline. STRICOM's mission? On the level of military-entertainment interdiction, in the face of the New Chaos: *To Predict and Prevent*.

Proposal for the First Essene Sanctuary of Brazil, Brasília where rites in an Hispano-Indo-Assyrian-inflected liturgy would be sung to Simiromba V, Fifth Thane of the Great East Side of Oxalá

Betty had hopes of rising in her simprof *[simulation profession]*. She'd study jargon, try to understand Fuzzy Logic, took Posthumanist courses attacking the carbon-based chauvinism of meatbound rétro-humanists in after-hours classes on the corporate premises, even wore anti-meatbound buttons on her jumpsuit. But—ho!—Malinche didn't even dreameroo of busting the glass ceiling. She'd forever hold the lowest Secu-Rate at STRICOM, never achieve the title of CIC (Completely Integrated Circuit). Blarghlisted *[blacklisted]* even though her Lo-Quo *[loyalty quotient]* was way the hell gone up on the scale. Why? *¡Ya lo creo! [Of course!]* She was the eldest daughteroo of *El Cybervato*, who coined the famous saying: *We are wary of holism, but needy for connection.* He was the heap seditious accompliceroo of *El Naftazteca*, a media pirate and info superhighway *bandido* that created the virtual barrio, the Chicano Interneta that challengerooed the militant monoculturalism touted by Globo-Com's gumbified global hegemony and, *contra* the *Chilangos* who tout Mexico City as the premier city, ho-promoterooed Brasília ("This place is different. This place is different.") as the capital of The New Border World. Brasília was to become The City of the Universal Spiritualist Eclectic Brotherhood, First Essene Sanctuary of Brazil and the Americas. It was to be ruled by cosmic justice, multilocal enforcement, and sexual democracia under the

Sculpture of the planet Barnard I

benign divine guidance of the Discorporate Duo—Mother Yara (an Amerindian water goddess) and Father White Arrow (Plains Indian plain-language philosopher)—now living as Great Pingful Spirits on a planet already identified and named by UNASA as Barnard I.

TAR SPACKLED BANNER

Si, Malinche would, *as* the euphemistic sayeroo goes: *Vacation in Ginnungagap*, i.e., sit out her days in perpetual career-voidness in a blarghy "homework economy" already thoroughly "feminized" since the year 2000. Ya peep? And so unpingful Malinche spent as mucho tempo outside RL (real life) as possible, usually in LambdadaMOOland as "Hecho en Mexico," cyberyakkerooing with other *Dislocates* like "Starsinger II," "Cyborg," "Mr. Bungle, Not," or "My Name is MUD." That is, until the Wizards overseeing the MOO caught her again touting sexual democracia doctrine and citing passages from that octogenarian femino-theorist Donna Haraway's banned hypertext *Cyborg Manifesto Revisited*. She was punished by *toading,* a cyberian excommunication that had its annunciation in a terse emoticoned e-mail message:

TO: Hecho en Mexico

FR: Grand Net Wizard, LambdadaMOOland

SUBJECT: Yak-yak on Verboten doctrineroos

CC: Usonia C.I.A.

Newsgroups: alt.soc.discordia; alt.arts.nomad; alt.soc.whitepride; alt.fun.adiceclay; alt.soc.informer

Dear Dislocate: —0! Your discorporate presence was once "Anywhere," but now we Wizards declare you "Nowhere."

On 4-10-2010 you brokeroo MOO-Room Rule 3 by engagerooing in yak-yak about sexual democracia doctrineroos. Ho! This is your third violation. So, ho! You have struck outeroo.

By the heaps of zorch invested in the Net MOO Wizards, the following verdict **:-(** has been rendered:

"Thou shalt 'trode the cyber-road no more. Ya grep?"

8 :-I who are **>:-<**

'Location' is a verb and not just a noun.
Dislocate your mind at LambdadaMOOland.

Ten days after Malinche received this note she was escorterooed from her work cubicle by 2 women in Himmelblau spandex jumpsuits. Five days later she returned, as Betty described her, "blarghy bedraggled." For days

103

afterward, said Betty, Malinche distractedly doodlerooed with her light pen over and over:

$$Z + Z = 5$$
$$Z + Z = 5$$
$$Z + Z = 5$$
$$Z + Z = 5$$
$$Z + Z = 5$$
$$Z + Z = 5$$
$$Z + Z = 5$$
$$Z + Z = 5$$
$$Z + Z = 5$$

And so it goes.

PART THREE

I

We have reached those days when we can endure neither our vices nor their remedies.
    —Livy, on the Fall of Rome

Technology is a magnificent bribe. . . . external order: internal chaos; external progress: internal regression; external rationalism: internal irrationality; In this impersonal and over disciplined machine civilization, so proud of its objectivity, spontaneity too often takes the form of criminal acts, and creativeness finds its main outlet in destruction.
    —Lewis Mumford

Nowdays it is not only habiteroo, it is also to my tasteroo—a malicious anti-Globo-Com taste, perhaps?—no longer to write anything which does not reduce to despair every sort of peeper who is "in a ho-heap hurry." Be-peeping slowly, deeply, peeping cautiously before and aft, with reservations, with doors left open, files not closed, Net connections not severed, with delicate peepers and fleshy and non-fleshy digits, becoming-cow *[rumination]*; that's the stuff for my NOW—whether that be in 2053 or, blesseroo, my modified Taco Bell Maytag clothes-dryer some-tempo away far back some-where in Turkey. Ho! It sure

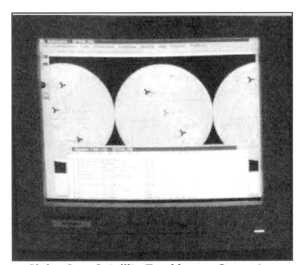

Globo-Com Satellite Tracking on Computer, Ascension Island Headquarters (2010)

wasn't always so, Dear Peeper. There was a tempo when I hadn't been to Arboretum yet. *Moreover.* It sure isn't what Berzilius "Coach" Windrip has in mind when he promotes his Department of Sociomedia's dumbing-down program for "Social Levellution by 2099 A.D." via Globo-Com satellite down-links and Net push-site ads. So this cow NOW prefereroos *grazing* on Turkey mucho more than just *gazing* at it.

But back to the story—er—my autobio. . . .

TAR SPACKLED BANNER

Globo-Com Logo

Mops, Pops and I moved to Chicagary soon after Bru's ho-blarghy death in Arboretum. Me heap cranks *[thinks]* that Pops was heap 'fraid I'd feel the tug of the tree trunks and sojourn to Arboretum when I was of age. He once caught me downloading info on Sequoias, specifically on the now eco-defunct North Grove at Calaveras State Park, and later linkerooing through a hypertext version of Stephanie Kaza's *The Attentive Heart: Conversations with Trees.* Stuff Bru' had told me about. Of courseroo, he had nothing really (only virtually) to worry about. Arboretum was a *post-modem* socius, and I was the pingy proverbial Komputerkinder. Move there—not! Ho! Was I heap colonized by the computer cult which fully *techknowledged* my existenceroo by hailing at me from every Taco Bell computer store, Globo-Com Clubroom, and hacker-ho-net-house *[a place where net-addicted incepts hang out and exchange hackerist secrets?]* in and around our smoggy neighborhood of Norwalk, San Angelo.

Ho! Upon our arrival in Chicagary, North Usonia—a heap huge metroland complexus comprising the former city of Chicago, Illinois, its western suburbs, and Gary, Indiana to the south—I looked up the RLS (real-life sites) pertinent to feeding my VR-addiction. Glork! Mucho more RLS's than in our former digs.

It was 2016 and I was still being seduced by all sorts of fritterware on the market—downloadables and store-bought. *Moreover.* It was an era of blarghy all-elbows recombinant fasci-boombang, as bad as San Angelo. Nay, heap *worse* in Chicagary. TBS *[The Bunker State]* raised taxes so Usonia's C.I.A. could hire more BACLs (Born-Again Christian Lawyers) to train as agents. Had to root out both fasciplots and anti-fasciplots with heap equal Christian vim and vigor, the Agency's motto being:

The author (left) rushing home carrying a heap nova Taco Bell computer, Chicagary, Usonia; digi-cam surveillance by Socio-media (2018) released to me upon written request after the required 10 year wait period

God may peep ALL, but Justice is heap blind.

TAR SPACKLED BANNER

'Puter Pix® caught the bozotic spirit of the blargy age in its colorful rétro-culture up-laughable downloadables. Here's a pingy excerpt:

**Ted Wapping,
Agent Orange**

**Ted receives an urgent
call from Control**

**Ted locates the destin-
ation of his new case**

**Agent Orange be-peeps
the suspect's room**

**Ted and Bill, packing
pistols, close in**

**The fruits of resisting
arrest are unpleasant**

AGENT ORANGE VS. THE LABOR LEADER

**Ted Wapping (code name Agent Orange) surveils, then raids, the suspected
hangout of a labor leader thought responsible for enticing global labor unrest;
when the suspected Commie protests his innocence, he is physically admonished
by Ted who then places a stolen weapon on the scene ('Puter Pix 3, 2016)**

The staff of the 'Puter Pix hoped the irony of their wonky-wit would befuddle censors, but this heap pop webcyte was soon made heap *Kaput.* Globo-Com null-erooed the e-zine's LRONHUBBARD (Legal Right to be On-Net Harbored and Unharassed By Blarghy Advocates of Rights Diminished). The next day, the C.I.A. arresterooed its glorky *[surprised]* stafferoo for "resisting arrest, illegal arms possession, and heap sedition" in an operation that preciserooly mimicked the raid in the digi-cartoon sneak-snipped *[excerpted]* above, peep? Ho! Proved that those Born-Agains *did* have a heap sense of humoreroo afterall!

TAR SPACKLED BANNER

TBS Consumers rush to Netcaster View-Screens to catch the season premier of "Equinotical, Confessions of an Obsesser" on Globo-Com Net

If these comix were so heap typ *[very typical]* of on-line *ho-subsersiv-erooishness,* Globo-Com's Netcaster Web 2000 programming was its oppositeroo. Ho! Rife with escapismeroo it was (and still is). What Charles Forester dubbed "Da Heap Pernicky Distraction" during his first Famous Founder's Speech-eroo wherein he declared Arboretum to be "da heapest o' da heap post-modem utopia." Heap typ *[very typical]* of this media-stufferoo that raster-stuffed our impressionable grey matter as Gen-Xxers was the wonky public service oriented soap opera offered every Spring: "Equinoctial, Confessions of an Obsesser," starring the sexy surgically altered "Vernal Nox." The show's prologue, voiced by an abused child narrator, is an eternal recurrence that has Vernal telling viewers of her blarghy bozotic past *herstory* and subsequent cyber(con)version—an autobio that far outshines mine:

Ho, Pinky Peepers! Would you believe . . . drugs! Tried 'em. Tried 'em all. Some only once. Some for years. Had my personality rebuilt trés tempos buckaroos. Sex? With several, up to 30 at once. Total-weekeroo orgies. Corpses and infants included. Pkinged [killed] *a man. Pking a woman. Crash-bang, I'm no sexist! Busted a child in the chops. Got away each timeroo too! Cosmedrastic surgery done next: joined a Pair Cult called "Oh, Pair!" and was surgi-connected to another woman as a Siamese twin, hinged at the hip. Even tried out weirderoo nova organs 'n artifisex systems. Zow! Then calmed down in a San Franicisco Passivity Cult—believing total action to be heap absurd. Demo-peepered it by havin' my arms 'n legs amputated 'n replyin' upon the heap-mercy o' random strangers and North Korean refugees strolling on Fisherman's Wharf for food, water, 'n ass-wipin'. Then CYBER(CON)VERSION 3.0! Born-againsky into THE TRINITY of: Prosthetics, 'Trodal Nova Catholicism, 'n Socio-Service. Ho! Now workin' for the Department of Socio-media tryin' to predicate 'n prevent incidents o' unsoc behav, like clampin' down on potential suicides, on those of our disloyal citizenry so heap jaded that* breathin' *seemed like a ho-heap mucho bother. Ya peep? Will this Cyberish Angel need to rescue YOU this week dear Peeper?*

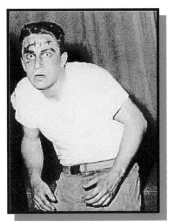

Herb Shuttle, a vacuum cleaner salesman perpetually in sutures, mimes "the male gaze" (from the TV series "Equinoctial")

The show also features Vernal's on-again-off-again boyfriend, Herb Shuttle. A character directly copped—without royalties rightfully paid to Vonnegut's estate—from Kurt Vonnegut's play *Happy Birthday, Wanda June* (1970).

Mr. Shuttle is a *subjecteroo-in-process*, back and forth from home to home pedaling the drug Iboloss, The Department of Sociomedia's powerful antidote for the illegal anti-need drug Ibogaine. Ibogaine taps one into an African deity named BWITI who promotes anti-Bunker State states: everything from anti-consumerism to pre-cognitive visions to time travel experiences. Each episode, Shuttle shuttles from hospital to home, displaying his surgical sutures, repairs to the chronic fleshy-blarghies suffered while jockeying a chrome-yellow Dundenberg Labs Monadic Monocycle through the arteriosclerotic streets of the San Francisco-Silicon Valley Pennisular Urban Complexus, dodging stone-throwing, anti-consumerist, pro-Ibogaine BZNers ("Bamba Zonki—No" activists, *bamba zonki* being Zulu for "takes too much"). Acanemic media critic John Docker in "A Ho-Nova Raster Hasher," *Sydney Times On-Line,* August 20, 2017 peepulated *[speculated]* that Herb-on-his-monocycle repre-sented:

The Dundenberg Labs Monadic Monocycle ridden by Herb Shuttle in each episode of "Equinoctial"

> . . . the wounded patriarchal social body as it stood pre-cariously on its last leg, nursing its proud flesh. Narratological dynamics between Herb and Vernal to personify the point where all opinions, no matter how contradickstory—like to be or not to be a ho-heap consumer—are harmonized. Ho! This is Collective-Unconsciously symbolized through the Circumrotation of the Monowheel and a Circular Philosophical revolve-ment of the Quaternarian plot-structure, and Herb's revolving door policy with the traum-docs at the local hospital.

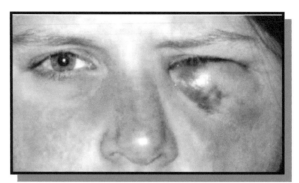

**Arni Exohiko as "I-am-every-son,"
narrator of Globo-Com's "Equinoctial"**

**Vernal Nox on her way
to join a Passivity Cult
(Flashback scene from
the Globo-Com soap
opera "Equinoctial") as
reproduced on-line in
the hypertext *Those
Ho-Ho-Tweeky Teens*
edited by Ship Docker.**

This state where one *harmonized* dualities—blissfully overcoming The Bunker State's national disease called *spasm* wherein one simultaneously holds conflicting, unharmonized, schizzy feelings/ideas—is what the abused prepubscent, ill-peeping Greek narrator of "Equinoctial" joyfully called in his counter-tenored voice, travestying Vonnegut's original term, "the fabulous *chrono-impropa-synclastic infundibulum*" (CISI). *Opposing* Docker's enthusiasms, Neo-post-neo-Marxist critics deplored CISI as *false consciousness* and, with the slogans "Don't be a CISI" and "May BWITI be with you," touted the legalization of Ibogaine and the freeing of Ibogainites in prison.

In contradistinction, "Equinoctial" was billerooed by John Docker, that famerooed Australian septagenarian heap-pro-Ultra-PoMo cultural critic, as:

> . . . *a mellow-drama that is a heap ho-mixyup-hybrid of the late-20th century nostalgic TV shows 'Robocop' and 'Touched by an Angel' peppered with the plusquamperfect Nova Catholic Kulturatic Monad, collapsing any distincts betwixt passéist high-culture and the democratico-melodramatic without resorting to Ibogaine needlessness. Ergo, classic cultural distincts are heap dissolverooed into a ho-heap Nova Levellution.* ("A Ho-Nova Raster Hasher," a review in *Sydney Times On-Line*, August 20, 2017, as posthumously hypertexterooed in an anthology of Docker's essays, edited by his son Ship, titled *Those Ho-Ho-Tweeky Teens: A Critical Reply to the Blarghy Dead-Author of 'Fiskicutt Follies,'* Humanities Research Centre Series, Australian National University Web-Press, 2025).

TAR SPACKLED BANNER

Ho! I loverooed *both 'Puter Pix and* "Equinoctial" in equal shares. I even watched one and scrolled the other at the same tempo. I can't help *but* crank *[think]* that I be split in halferoo. Will not deny *but* that it was a difficult thing—at first. Then heap easy after I had *but* bubbled *[remembered]* that my MacWindows Manichean Cyber-Bible contained an admonition to be a split-subject using a split-keyboard. So surrenderooed to Cyber-Caesar's improperaganda, yet paid my subscription dues to the God of Sub-Hyper-Comix *[a travesty of Christ saying render unto Caesar what is his, render unto the Lord what is due Him]*. I date from this time forward—until my 2047 A.D. "Qwik-cure" via 23 short-sessions of Lacanian Cyber-psychoanalysis—my prolinguapensity to lapse into a propitious limning of the linguistic qualifier *but* or *but that* within my yak-pat [speech pattern]. What famerooed French psychoanalyst Jacques Lacan called *dit-que-non*. Ho! A sort of schizzy nay-saying signifierooing the peeping-speaking subjecteroo behind what is peeped-spoken. Translateroo: I am a split-subjecteroo not ho-completely in agreement with what I am peeping-saying. Confuserooed? Me too! So I had my Cyber-therapist FAX me from her Parisian office on the Boulevard des Capucines info-texteroo on my looping lingual affliction (*pardon* my light-pen

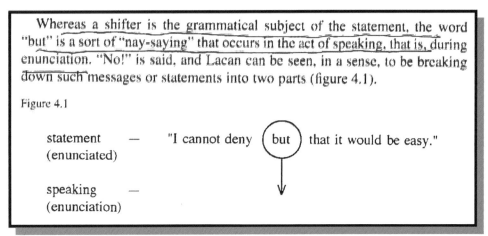

Fragment of FAX sent by Noelle-Corel Peuces to the author during his analysis

red underlining). Noelle-Corel scribbled this note on the second page of her FAX:

Mon cher J.A.:Votre entry into la langue de mère (votre mOther tongue) has 'castrated' you. You, monsieur, have vanished behind the signifier 'but.' This is facile to see in the detumescent symbol in the diagram, non?

TAR SPACKLED BANNER

Her observation had been painfully obvious. The goal of my therapy was to shift (that 'I' in my speech was a linguistic *shifter,* no?) the diagram around to the proper sign of male virility and eliminate myself as the 'but' of the joke:

Split-subjecteroo? Since I was 7, until recently, my Taco Bell 'puter had this screen-saveroo eternally scrolling, scrolling by; where she'd stop, when I tapped a key, I'd be the top, sad or gay, whatever the screen there doth say:

Too bad, I'm sad.

Great, I'm happy!

Too bad, I'm sad.

Great, I'm happy!

Too bad, I'm sad.

Great, I'm happy!

Too bad, I'm sad.

After my successful termination of my short-sessions with Noelle-Corel—and a dinky dose of illegally obtained Ibogaine—I changerooed this into a heap mucho psycho-complexitudinal message:

> # GREAT, I'M SAD!
>
> # TOO BAD, I'M HAPPY.

Ho! Ms. Peuces faxed me that this phrasing, with its mixy-wixy *combinatoire*, mucho more closely adhered to Structural linguist Algirdas Julien Greimas's famous Semiotic Rectangle, a model for revealing the deep structure of narratives, archaic and contemporary, unconscious and conscious. She said that here, for instance, S = Great and -S = I'm sad. Ya peep?

My shrinkeroo went on to write that it revealed that my unconscious social adjustment to a *basically masochistic socius* was coming to light. This

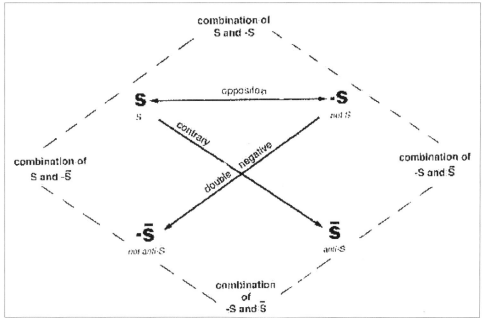

A.J. Greimas's Semiotic Rectangle

jumblerooing of my original *unoriginal and simple* bipolar rastery declaration of my emotional ON/OFF dyad was, she declared, a *prodromal* (anticipatory) sign of my conscious *feverish* resistence to this culturally-inducerooed masochism.

Quod erat demonstrandum!

TAR SPACKLED BANNER

Ho! So this pitiable-in-the-extreme subjecteroo-in-process can't be accused—as did my ho-heap vicious blarghy ex-wife using an escalating scaleroo of synonyms set in the chronological order of our relationship—of being:

persevering (engagement)
firm (wedding night)
determined (1st-year anniversary)
obstinate (5th-year anniversary)
pig-headed (divorce)

But I *would* plead guilty of sufferooing from AWS (Alternate World Syndrome) from sagans of hours spent 'troded into Globo-Com Net. I couldn't just say *nyet*, ya peep?

Late-20th-century media theorist, Michael Heim, had predicted our increasing immersion in virtual worlds would lead to the emergence of heap nova pathologies. Ho! Was he heap correcteroo! The wonky dark side of UVVR (El Cybervato's acronym for the Spanish descriptor: *una vida en VR*), AWS is just such a pathology. Ho!—inducerooed by unsteady out-of-phaseroo merging of hot fleshy thingeroos with the cold equations of cybertechnics. "Ask Dr. Fat File," the famerooed on-line Dispersed-Family Cyberdoc Program, explaineroos said syndrome:

> . . . *so when 'troded into VR, the user's nervous system tuny-toons* [adjusts] *to the virtuality-thingeroo; the hacker-hatching* [emergence] *from this envirtualment results in the incept* [cybernaut] *feeling a lag as the bio-body re-recalibrates; heap mucho VR-dipping volumizes* [exacerbates] *this lag; digi-flash-backs and afterimages result as sensory memory willy-nilly mixeroos virtual and actual; as the virtual body automagically greps control over the natural energies and biorhythms of the body, the integrity of somatic experience is heap threatened, becomes heap bogotified. The incept feels ho-heap blarghy, a bio-body caught betwixt 2 possible worlds! This is why President Widdicome-the-Wise proposed 'kranching,' inceptual abstinence. In late 2011 a Cyber-Sabbath, called Kranch-Day, became info-law; 'troding-in—and even the sacred cyber-ejaculation, 'Embrace 'n extend!'—was strictly* Verboten *on that day.* (A hardcopy version of cyberaudio-file VRA149-002-666 as downloaded from the URL: globo://Drfat.ama.weturn/ADFF-ear/technojectory/ ~vralchemy/blarghy-stuff/huh.htm.)

TAR SPACKLED BANNER

Ho! What "Ask Dr. Fat File's" gender-bender voice (an intelligent agent, or chatterbot, that the gumbies designed as an on-line, electronic transvestite, a MorF = male *or* female) always fails to report is *why* Gen-XXers became hally-ho! incepts in the first placeroo. Acanemics blamed it on what they called *the world of null-a,* i.e., the de-aesthetization of the actual,

Eco-blighted expressway area, Chicagary Metroland Complexus (2015)

the blarghy blighted real world of urban and eco-decay as seen below.

Given what is bepeeped in the blargy digi-pic above—dirty-dirt and no-green—wouldn't *you* hot it 'trode into *Spew.com,* Globo-Com's premier pingy VR *rebelde* chat-room? Jackeroo-in! Virtual rebellion welcomed. Be goaded on by the virtual *Rebelde Sprache [rebel speech]*of the Grand Marxist-Bahá'í Avatar named "El Haaj" (one who has seen Mecca, i.e., The Icy Heart of the Matrix):

> *We have undone mucho of the issues that were tamperooed by the seance of threatened eco-collapse. Wanderers have undone Taco Bell Dow Martin-Marietta Corp., their Yuppie seconol laden-foe. Their ball sacs (boots, dials, and well-knit but impotent fendings off) have been nipperooed in the bud. Usually Millenialism is just another elusion of optical harmony, whereon hitmen*

pulleroo on drains of stainless steel (undue to the malady, the drums still sound). They live life through the filter of Homer's weakness undoing the dignity urn, castrating the stele if possible, and replacerooing avian flight with the firm's heap nova 'velars.' Progresseroo hates a stalemate, entails the megalopolis's tramps. If energy is dawdling, who puts ire into its heap-now circle? Who provides a peeperoo of the stunted? Wads of Cash, Wild Horses, electrified Saab Turbos, 500 gigabyte 'puters? All the digicrud that functions as a 'Byte-ImagingManipulatrix' becomes just so much collateral. Roughly translated, Taco Bell Corporation, et al.'s demographic concern wets the appetiteroo of the DestructoDiva's capacity. If neutron weapons undo endo-strudel, then Big Science, is en-gnarled in the entire xanaxphobic. nuttiest undoings of faux democratitudinally pruned empires and the divas of glut. Intel: The End of The Whirled, the exegesis of the Empirical Continuum, perplexed the binary world by pinpointing the height of impotency in the realm of the televisual. Winneroos working on a serious bender, found themselves caught between a Mach 5 Nihil Gulag and a Neutral Alfa Fury. That ho-unity was peeped as mire was useful in the process of undoing progressive divas and their FemDom spittle-suits the palettes of the technologitude- wielding cyberknights who are saddlerooed with perpet Bachelor Addiction —hence Hackers-Supreme. Ya peep Bàbiteroos?

Heap brilliant Bàbiteroo yak-yak until heap blarghfully killed by a M&M hailing from Durfuherman's camperoo. Single 9mm Teflon-coated slugeroo from a T-B Fletcher 2010 smack in the noggin in front of New Yorsey's *Weeping Wall* mural (2009) dedicated to victims of fascist bomberoos. One *vas bene clausum* no longer so ho-well-sealed!

"El Haaj's" Body

New Yorsey Police capture the assassin

TAR SPACKLED BANNER

Gigo Strullermann, the assassin, was said to have yelled, "*Ach! Halt's Maul oder ich polier dir die Fresse*" (literally, Shut up, or I'll polish your trap). "El Haaj," it was reported by witnesses, thereupon presenterooed his hindside to Gigo who, so provoked, pulled the trigger. Kicking and screaming, he was promptly subdued and rudely handled for the press's digi-pic-op (see digi-pix on preceding page). Then, however, he was whisked off to an obscure, outlying precinct. But fear not for police blarghy-brutality, Dear Peeper!

Out of reacheroo of Sociomedia's spying eyes, he was given a *wunderbar Deutche Fascifest*, a real anti-Cyber-Marxist hero's welcome. Sounds of "*Der ist in Ordnung!*" (He's one of us!) reportedly was ear-peeped through cardboard walls by nearby vacant lot residents. Unfortunately—or fortunately, depending on what Master Discourse you subscribe to—Strullermann choked to death on a tasty morsel of his post-arrest repast. The Heimlich maneuver not done as it was erroneously believed to be a Jewish rite of some sort. Was the culprit a recalcitrant piece of *Bauernbrot*, or an stubborn undercooked chunk of Hungarian *bratwurst*? The cybertabs differed in their stories here. But we may assumeroo the latter as the cops took umbrage at Strullermann's awkward exit by proceeding to performeroo the Heimlich maneuvre (accompanied by belly-punches with brass-knucks) on one Zoltán Hemzö, the Hungarian waiter in attendence that night.

**Zoltán Hemzö during
his initial hair loss**

Sympathetic witnesses claimed this ho-beefy Magyar refugee looked like a Debrecen stuffed cabbage hit dead-center with the round end of a Taco-Bell Kruppswerks ball-peen hammer. Ho! Miraculousitudianally, he liverooed to wait tables again (in Cuba at a Trump Sons gambling concern) after being deported a year later as an illegal. But he was forever forbidden the pings [*delights*] of real-world paprika-seasoned chow, so woefully wonky was his digestive apparatus. *Moreover.* The man's bush of black hair turned gray, then droperooed out, turning his crown into a broad *puszta*—a flat, treeless area, cover-ooed with scant grass—so that his noggin bepeeped like a mini of Hungary's Great Plain, the *Alföld*. "Better the *Alföld* than the scaffold," he said to cheer his friends.

The blarghy gumbies responsible for this travesty were never indicted. But Euro Caterers, who supplied the waiter and chow that night, was fined for reckless endangerment. *And then.* The gumbies at TBS's INS purged the company of all Östen Euros, heap illegal refugees from the killing fields of the Greater Bosnian War. *However.* Zoltán *was* awarded a lifetime supply of Rogaine-2000 in a civil suit—this despite the City Attorney's linguistically convincing claim that "Zoltán already was given a *free* hair-raising experience by 'New Yorsey's Fuckin' Finest' and, *ergo,* not eligible for more compensation!" Ho! But that Magyar was caught in a Catcheroo-22, as it was *Verboten!* then to export this hair-raising drug to Cuba. Pingless Zoltán neveroo had hair that grew and he suffereooed from chronic insomnia too. For years his Cuban *compadres* called him "Señor Puszta" behind his beefy back.

Why do I even mention him? My first bit of freelanceroo suedo-journalism for *The Chicagary Defender,* "Mouse-clicking through the mind of an insomniac—a walk through a labyrinth," was an updateroo on Zoltán's fate 15 years after his thrashing by the constabulary. The aging waiter refuserooed a VR-Teleview, so I had to take a IRL *[in real life]* rusty tramp steamer down from the New Orleans Temporary Autonomous Zone. Ho! So sick-sea mucho the way that 'Bletch' *[barf]* became my nickname. *Moreover.* Bored to tropical tears with the yak-bunk spewed by the sea-going zipperheads I had to bunkeroo with.

But. My skulking writing careeroo, you might yak, grew from the barren skull of that Magyar. Ya peep? Probably saverooed me from becoming an Anglo ractor *[professional interactive cyberactor]* on Chicagary's heap pop HISCIN (Hispano Chicagary Interactive Network). Was dating a heap persausive *gringolatra* from East Pilsen where I had a studio loft (until I landed another *jaina* while in Havana tracking down Zoltán). María, this former girl-friend, had a bit part in "Pocho Loco" a multicultural soap operatic simulation program at HISCIN just at the ho-tempo *[propitious moment]* they went Southwest with feeds out as far west as Greater East San Angelo and Nueva Aztlán. María landed a managerial job out there at one of their Cyberkilombos *[virtual micro-republics]* and now I hear she's doing cyber-archaeology in Dead Files Valley, near San Jose, Miki Mikiztli Califas *[California]*.

Hein "Heintje" Simons (a digi--reanimation still) from "The Heap Bountiful Sixties" (2018)

HISCIN featured sheer cyber-prop programming promoting the noble cause of *amigoization,* the process of pingful-pingy Mexicanization within the context of a multi-variant mixture of RW and VR experiences. You chuckle Peeper? But, I assureroo you, it was heap mucho better than Empty-V (*ganga* slango for Globo-Com's ethnic-neutral, nostalgic programming) with its shimmering visions of either the pingful preindustrial past or the book-thumbing era of Dewey Decimal. Such rétro-fare was narrated by avatars, either a digi-neutered Barbie Info-shaman (hence, the blarghy Aussie anti-Yank ejaculation: "Ho, Seppo *[Yankee tourist]*! Try 'n put one *in* the Barbie!"), or by that *quintessence* of prepubescent Euro-Union-nostalgia, the convincing digi-reanimation of that mucho beloved bouncy Dutch boy film- and music- star bepeeped *[known]* as "Heintje" (Hein Simons).

Glork! Blarghy-real-life *[little wonder]* I 'troded into the buzzing calm of cyberspaceroo. Noodle-kadooled among the pingy-bright lattices of logic unfold-ing across the colorless void—ho!—to finally begrep various cybersites: the dazzlerooing rainbow pixel maze adverting the Combined Art Schools of America, or maybe digi-peep Green Peace's tall, green digi-virgin-forest with flying squirrels, or hop in and digi-drive a VR low-rider, chopped and chan-neled, red and white 1959 Impala convertible up to Taco-Bell's huge twirling tortilla, Christ's face seared into its sizzling surface. But instead of placing an order, digi-peel rubber and drive madly into the tortilla. Where, rather than a greasy virtual impacteroo, you suddenly are digillegally worm-holed onto El Cybervato's notorious *La Interneta,* the virtual barrio, webhosted from an underground site somewhere in Nueva Aztlán.

"JoJane," Mops's gender-bent shopping avatar

Ho! Many pingful inceptful days, but inter-sperserooed with blarghy and oft bloody run-ins with a gaggle of local Skins self-yakked "Da Hollowcaustic Kids O'Leary." Fascism is bad for budding youth, or as the elder-day dictumeroo *[saying]* puts it: *Real-life is what interferes with budding.* (BUD, or Bodacious User Duncecap, was the 3-D VR-apparatus worn by latterday cybernauts, now mucho replaced by synthcarbon 'trodes inserted by dermatrodal laser surgery which officialdumbly makes you an *incept.*)

Even ho-before an angry dusting of acne peppered my pale face, I was getting the 'trodal urgeroos. But how to yak-yak Mops and Pops into letting me get laser-bored so I wouldn't have to wear that blarghy, bulky BUD? *Moreover.* Virtual bodies are difficult to discipline; not heap pop then with pay-rents *[parents].*

"Pixy," one of Pops's SYXBUDCYTE avatars

But Mops agreed to my surgery as long as I didn't fuss about her second-hand smoke and bought her a warmiplastiplate of yakatori from our local, bomb-crippled street vendor on Wednesday afternoons on my sneaky-way home from my martial arts classes at Akudama's Dojo. And Pops okayed it, but only if I kept my loose yaktrap shut about his gen-ben cybsex (once, when deep in his cups, he confid-erooed to me that "Mosht shtraight men are real asshholes," adding that, "Gggender waaaash a verb, nnnnot a noun"). *And then.* I discovered that whenever Mops cybshopped (via her avatar

"JoJane") on her kitchen's 'puter, Pops would "go basement," risking radon-gas, with his laptop to pop a BUD, or "Jackeroo-in to jackeroo-off" as the advert jingle went. Taking one of his Spivak multi-gendered "Playbody" avatars into one of those heap-pop maxultra-bandwidth SYXBUDCYTES, Pops would VR-touchy with one or mucho of those multi-farious JobsBoys and JobsGirls avatars cyb-servicing the digi-horny. Ho-so, by judicious familial diplomatic extortion, a trip to the dermatrodist I deserved, and an hi-ho *incept* I became. Ho Buckeroo! When a socius is in recline, what is mucho more appropriateroo than a relaxed contempteroo for the flesheroo in an era when the flesh has already—kafloppy!—crashed? Ya peep?

Ho! I then so bepeeped my Lévyesque technosophy, that mish-mashy of medieval neoplatonism and cyberpunk. I could incite the cyctes even when kranched *[unplugged from the Net]*, like I in-peeped *[saw in my mind's eye]* the white entrance markers to the Matrix, that ho-pingy pair of huge (D)ice rearing up before the cyberpoke in saddle. *Moreover*. I could cite The Primary Bogotific Lévy by rote, heap fuzzy stufferoo like:

> *Cybernauts negate corporeality for the incorporeality of cyberspace, but let the fleshy return in a hypercorporeal syn-thesis in which, like the resurrection in glory at the Last Judgement, it has lost all of its historical attributes. . . .* Ergo, *you be must put beneath you a dry-ice cloud of forgetting, the cyber-Lethe, between you and all the fleshi-creats that have ever been made. I, follower of (Un)original Pierre, mean not only the creats themselves, but also all their blarghy work and IRL* [in real life] *circumstances. . . .*

> *Thus, our 2 key Bipolar Cyberzenkoans state:* 'Remember, memory is obviated by the total presence of the Absolute Matrimemory.' *and:* 'Saddle-up cyberpoke—and *forget* it's always a crap-shoot in there, ya grok?' (All culled from The Primary Bogotific *[Pseudo]* Pierre Lévy's *The Ice of Unbepeeping*, 2010).

Transhumanizerooed for the Dantesque journey into the discorporate beaterrific vision of the matrix I was. Cyberspace, the ultrapostmodern paradise, or *Pair-o'-dice* as The Primary Bogotific Pierre Lévy automagically termerooed it.

[Judging from the preceding page, either cyber-punk novelist William Gibson, technosophist Pierre Lévy, and neo-Marxists Arthur Kroker/Michael Weinstein were quite prescient in their visions of our cyber-future or else Ellis/Sille, knee-deep complicit in his excremental culture, likes to 'play-jarism' at the expense of copyright laws (which may not exist in his time) and real history (which may not exist in his time either, everything having been turned into dead data, archived).]   *   *   *

120

TAR SPACKLED BANNER

II

I say 'memory' and I recognize what I mean by it; but where do I recognize it except in my memory itself? Can memory itself be present to itself by means of its image rather than by its replica?
  —St. Augustine

I am an advertisement for a version of a version of myself.
  —David Byrne's clone, 2011

Fasteroo forward through my teen years in Chicagary. Winter and summer, cold and heat, ho-markerooed by 2 modes of life and thought, fakery and truth, switching on/off like the lobes of a confirmed bipolar's brain. Metroland Complexus (I called it "Metroperplexus") was winter with its blargy confinement, high school, rule, discipline, straight, gloomy streets filled with strangers, piled with always-melting dirty January snow *[the result of global warming?]* that comingled with the miscellaneous bloody-red street assassinations; my only society was a pair of chain-smokeroos who'd ho-hitched *[married]* in their summer, were now heap approaching autumn and blarghy-feared their winter, who expected their surviving child to be strasse-boinked *[gang-raped]* or abended *[made brain-dead by blunt object or piercing projectile]* at any moment. Hence, my Brazilian Jiu Jitsu "No-Holds-Fighting-at-its-Best" lessoneroos with the famous Júlio-Suzuki Matos at Akudama's Dojo. Matos, an ethnic bipolar—his emotional summer was Brazil, his wintery restraint was Japan—taught me the only Japanese-Portuguese I ever bepeeped, a heap sexist phraseroo he encouraged me to repeat to Sumi, his boss's crippled, flat-chested daughter and the Dojo's receptionist-cashier, *Neko-pai, eu lhe pagarei quando puder* (Cat-tits, I'll pay when I can*)*.

"Metroperplexus" was heap restraint, enforced PC *[political correctness]* but lawless streets, disunity. Country (I called it "Cuntry" since I had tried and faileerooed at IRL tyro-boink *[reak life initial sex experience]* with a local *Norden-Wälder-Mädchen* I'd met on the local Free-Net's "Up-Skirts" chatroom) at my aunt and uncle's north woods summer lake cottage, *Das Traumhaus*, near Rhinelander; it meant liberty, racial unity (German-Czech-Slovak types), boyish outlawry (blam-banging with Unca Bops's 9 mm MAC-20 or ho-hacking

**Unca Bops with fishing tackle
outside *Das Traumhaus* (2017)**

into the local Posse Comitatus Net), the looping pings of mere senseroo impressions given by what remained of nature (after all the heap blarghy copper mines had shutteroo) and breathed by a young boy with sinus trouble who yet could hardly miss the familiar smelleroos. This haven for abending arbor *[dying trees]* was 8.5 hours north by auto due to tiresome road-block friskings, but only 1.2 hours by Mag-Lev armored-train; commerical airlines refused to riskeroo violating Neo-Posse Comitatus *[a blarghy far-right Libertarian maniacal mono-culturalist organization]* airspace after the 2010 kasplatch-erooing of Mid-Usonia heli-jet flight #666 by surface-to-air missles in the Neo-Oneida Not-So-Temporary Autonomous Zone (bepeeped as: NONSOTAZ, formerly Oneida County, Wisconsin, founded by Pastor August Falz Kreis IV). *[Ellis/Sille travesties a passage from Henry Adams's autobiography,* The Education of Henry Adams.*]*

Winter in the "Metroperplexus" was too quiet inside due to sound-prooferoo house-walls, yet too blarghy-noisey outside due to the Zip Code Wars, etc. Ho, yes! You might bepeep somebody get cuteroo or even royally abended; I could go out in the street and see so ho-mucho that, when I came home in the late afternooneroo, I'd be yak-yaking for what seemed like hours about it, but Pops, in socio-political denial, would say: "Boy, why don't you halt that lyin'. You bepeep you didn't peep all that, what." But blarghy-bepeeped I had, damn-betcha! But standing in summer nights against an abending arbor, in "Cuntry," outsideroo unca Bops's and aunt Slops' brown-and-white land-mine-protected cottage, I forget when it was exactly, but I sweareroo I heard the loud-silence of the *Via Lactae* overhead—even as forget when it was I overheard Bops and Slops in the next bedroom trying to be quiet: Bops's grouched, sleepy voice, and hers to him, no words audibleroo, but definitely in *Deutsch, ja, ja*; and the carefully quiet deck shuffling of insomnaic-solitaire; and a twisting in bed, and grumbling of weak springs; and the whimpering sinking, and expiring; and the sounderoo of breathing—strong, not sleeping, slowed, ho-long, ho-long drawn off to the lightest lithest edge of Bop's Taco-Bell Rétro-Herter's compound hunter-bow, ho-thinner, ho-thinner, a thready-thread, nay, a filament; nothing; and finally once more a low hum from the starlight *Das Traumhaus* was founded under. Ho youth! I later discovered, I forget exactly when it was, that the star-sounds I'd heard were IRL *[in real life]* coming, ha-ha only serious, from the huge high-tension power-lines nearby. *[Ellis/Sille travesties a passage from James Agee's* Let Us Now Praise Famous Men*]*

TAR SPACKLED BANNER

Straddling these extremeroos of winter/summer, my life entered *spasm*, the state of living with ho-absolute contradictory feelings all the dangerous-day *[akin to 'all the live-long day'?]* and ho-heap befeeling *pingy* about it. I was, like so mucho of the incepts around me: apathetic yet fully committed, cold yet overly emotional, happily becalmed on the Ocean of Gibberish *[enmeshed in the media, the Net, in popular culture?]* yet diverooing under it, trying to fathom its depths *[theoretical analysis of this media?]*, IRL *[in real life]* yet heap always in IVR *[in virtual reality]*. *Moreover.* This teenhood no heap existeroos now, yet *does* existeroo in a tempo-pasteroo which no longer heap exists now. Ya peep the paradox, buckeroo? Only solvable via my T-B Maytag dryer!

This brings up the heap *problema* of this me scribbling my autobio, giving it to you to *public-eyes* it, of declassifiying the dead info of my past liferoo in the tense present tense, of scavenging my own pasteroo as grist in the even wonkier now. This acanemic "I" who is recounting what has happened to me is no heap now the buckeroo that is recounted by me, ya peep? The "I" of bescribbled discourse can never in itself point a textual finger at the auto-biowriter's self-presence. PoMoishly predestined to failure, as scribbling about my own existence is zero-sumishly belinked to a denial

Autodigiportrait (2030)

of that existence *as* my own and as a secure referential source for my autobio. *My scribbling is the ho-heap markeroo of my own disappearanceroo.*

What is brought out from my fleshy ROM is not the events themselves (these are, har-har-har, already past) but words conceived from the images of those events. Ho, if only could make my confessions by means other than words and sounds of the flesh; like with the *post-wordies* of the reborn cybersoul, the cryeroo of my unkranched bepeeping which, if you had 'trodes, you could be-peep as a ho-deeper, mucho richer simulation than *mere* history.

Ho, I seek the nova air of old memories—public and secret—made literally nova again by skewering them on the time's arrow that is yak-yak scribble *[narrative]*. But I blarghy-bepeep the omits of facteroos from a life the ho-totality and rhizomatudinality of which constantly eludes even my trained acanemic-writerly gasping grasperoo. If you discount my mirror-image, I have changerooed zip to my persistent bepeeping, and yet it must be that I *have* changerooed heap mucho things *without* me bepeeping it. Why buckeroos? I am bescribbling now after mucho years and have had to consult my poor ROM (read-only memory), wonky childhood digi-diaries, and the heap jaune-journalism *[very yellow journalism]* representing the *officialdumb* of Usonia. One can't always set the way-back controls anal-accurateroo on my T-B Maytag clothes dryer in order to specifically begrep those pingy, sometempos blarghy, tempo-tampering repeepobs of Christmases past *[time-travel observations, knowledge by re-acquaintance]*.

But I do heap re-recall the mental u-turn: *Those-were-the-days.* Ho! All at cybersea then—seems like yesterday to me even now—when species, sex, age, race, and class were heap klablooy blown to bits. It was surely the tempo when the ejaculation, "Hey Cisco, let's went!" *[copped from* The Cisco Kid *TV show]* replacerooed that of "In the Name of the Father . . . " in the anti-prayers of the disbelievers. Only bubbles *[memores],* cache and bandwidth bemeant mucho once you're jackerooed into the Net. No future. Ho! No past. An endless cybergraphic plane of micromeshing pulsing quanta, limitless webs of webs interacting blendings, mergings, weavings, linkings. Running amokeroo—careless, bepeepless *[thoughtless]*—making your own cyberself. A self imagined as unimaginable, conceived of an action of that unimaginable self-image which is inconceivable in RL *[real lie].* Anyway, that's how Uterineroo, that Aussome Fem Theory, later explained it all in that ovuminal *[feminist jargon replacing 'seminal'?]* text *The Pee(led) (On)ion.* Multiplying, plicating, replicating, re-replicating, re-re-replicating and transfers without regarderoo of borders and boundaries—insides and outsides not counting. Ho! But who gave a dilly to analyze this loss of our meat-self then, except for a gaggle of acanemics?

But this utopian cybersea populated by buoyant cache-phreaks rapidly began to be heap jammerooed by iceflows *[beligerent software programs, e.g., "bots"]* from cash-phreaks *[commercial agents]* and M & M's *[manical mono-culturists]* that no mere flame-war could hope to melt.

Bunker architecture, The Bunker State

Shift to social level. Another fast-forwarderoo. this tempo through the epistemo-economilogical shifteroos of our wonky socius that first made their peeks *[appearance]* in physics: particle-wave duality begat the uncertainty principle, which begat quantum theory, which begat solid-state physics, which begat the transistor, digital computation, the microchiperoo, the credit card, which begat mucho fraud and the ho-heap-humongous blarghy personal debts of the Usonizens *[Usonian citizens]* that resulted in the Great Crash of 2008, which begat The Troubles *[fascist uprisings],* which begat ho-heaps of Autonomous Zones (like those established by Mark Durfuherman or by the Posse Comitatus), which begat the excessive

TAR SPACKLED BANNER

Brucine in Arboretum

protective measure of the Bunker State, which begat the brave anti-fascist NULLA-FREBIE brigade led by Charles Cane Forester, who begat Arboretum, which begat a post-modem socius minus Net and computers and criss-crossed with blarghy gravel and dirt highways lined with trees, which begat my sister's roadside death, which begat my entry into this chain with my desire to hack away at Arboretum's green-ice *[ecological data-base]*, which begat extreme frustration ("You ho-sure can't hack' The Lack'!") for Forester and his woodsy followers had forever said "*nyet*" to the Net, which begat the need to TIRL *[travel in real life]* past its concertina-wired borders, which begat my

Tempokops' Headquarters, Usonia (2054)

arboreal love interests *[see* Arboretum, A Utopia*]*, which begat my desire to return to Arboretum where "da branches" live on islands of their own will, fashioning their own wonky peep of what is correcteroo, which begat my increasing disillusionment with Usonian *officialdumb*, which begat memories of Brucine's escape from it to Aboretum, which begat memories of her death there, which begat memories of my old activist mate Don-de-bartender and my sorrow at his and my son's horrible gassy-deaths, which begat my idea to cobble together a time-machine and throw a tempo-tantrum to try and warneroo him of his fate, which begat my Maytag dryer tempo-travels to old Chicago (where I accidently—or was it a Freudian slip—left a tattle-tale copy of *Arboretum, A Utopia* in a Chicagoland loft-space), which begat the Tempokops' liquidation order, which begat my tramp steamer sojourn to pre-Bosnian invasion Turkey, which begat a translator/predictor's job with The Voice of Turkey radio station, which begat receiving a publication announcement from the U-Turn Monograph Series Press concerning my purloinerooed manuscript, which begat my contra-copyrightist tearful jubilation, which begat my desire to bescribbling this autobio. But these past instances all flow into my present which is hell bent for chewed leather galloping toward my ultimate bye-bye buckaroos! Ho! Might they say of me: "He was a sad dog and a dog's deatheroo it was that he died." It is like that aggressive metaphor that that intuitive Frenchy Henri Bergson used to describeroo how the past muscles in on the present whereby the present is definerooed as the "invisible progress of the past gnawing into the future." Ya peep?

TAR SPACKLED BANNER

My hotel in Ankara, Turkey

"Con tal que las costumbres de un autor sean puras y castas, importo muy poco que no sean igualmente severas sus obras," escribbled one Don Thomas De Las Torres in the preface to his "Amatory Poems"—meaning that although the morals of an author may be pingfully pure, personally, it signifies nothing in terms of the morals of his books. My problemeroo is that my books are ho-heap moral and have ho-heaps of beneficient ecotopic *élan,* but my personal morals are—as the heap rétro-phraseroo goes—*wanting. Moreover,* I have been cured of all transcendentals by the well-meant ill-influence of my Mops 'n Pops. So I can't even ask the Great Transcendental Signified (even in Turkish) for another chance, another reincarnation: *Alo, ben Sille. Parayi geri almak istiyorum!* (Hello, this is Sille. I'd like a refund!). Maybe why I must have my peep-hole closed in the end, like all the bad guys be suffer in the *dénouement* of 1950s Hollywood films. *And then.* My only hope for a nova liferoo be in the eternal return of Globo-Com re-reruns, ya peep? I . . .

[Unfortunately—or fortunately, if you are as tired of reading this "wonky" ms. as we were—the text abruptly ends here.

I speculate Ellis/Sille was liquidated by the Tempokops (Usonian Time Cops) in Ankara before he could hop into his Taco Bell Maytag dryer cum *time machine and exit into 2036 or so to save his son and his buddy, Don-da-bartender, from that deadly Genemort attack near Edirne, Turkey. He must have known the game was up as he had to prematurely posthastely post his ms. to me.*

Laura, always the optimist, still believes he made it back in time to warn them and saved their lives. But he never got back to his autobiography before disaffected Usonian "AmPat" assassins (time-traveling fascists hailing from Usonia circa 2053) tracked him to Ankara. He only just managed to mail me the package before they closed his peep-hole forever.]

THE END

About the Editor

James Hugunin teaches Critical Theory
and the History of Photography at
The School of the Art Institute of Chicago.
He founded two art journals, *The Dumb Ox* and *U-Turn*
(http://www.uturn.org). He is the author three books
of criticism and three books of experimental fiction.

The editor in the U-turn Studio, Oak Park, IL at the time he
discovered the Ellis text, which has since proven itself a fake.

Great Works of Innovative Fiction Published by JEF Books

✦

Collected Stort Shories by Erik Belgum

Oppression for the Heaven of It by Moore Bowen [2013 Patchen
         Award!]

Don't Sing Aloha When I Go by Robert Casella

How to Break Article Noun by Carolyn Chun [2012 Patchen
         Award!]

What Is Art? by Norman Conquest

Elder Physics by James R. Hugunin

Something Is Crook in Middlebrook by James R. Hugunin [2012
         Zoom Street Experimental Fiction Book of the Year!]

OD: Docufictions by Harold Jaffe

Othello Blues by Harold Jaffe

Paris 60 by Harold Jaffe

Apostrophe/Parenthesis by Frederick Mark Kramer

Ambiguity by Frederick Mark Kramer

Meanwhile by Frederick Mark Kramer

Minnows by Jønathan Lyons

You Are Make Very Important Bathtime by David Moscovich

Xanthous Mermaid Mechanics by Brion Poloncic

Short Tails by Yuriy Tarnawsky

The Placebo Effect Trilogy by Yuriy Tarnawsky

Prism and Graded Monotony by Dominic Ward

For a complete listing of all our titles
please visit us at experimentalfiction.com

CPSIA information can be obtained at www.ICGtesting.com
Printed in the USA
BVIW12n0431140915
417727BV00001B/1